IN SEARCH OF ANCIENT

Atlantis

by Phillip Gregoire

Printed and bound in the United States of America
First printing • ISBN # 978-0-9908913-9-0
Copyright © 2016

Cover Photo of Erwin Rommel by Bundesarchiv, Bild 146-1973-012-43 /
Unknown / CC-BY-SA 3.0

This is a work of fiction. Names, characters, businesses, places, events and
incidents are either the products of the author's imagination or used in a
fictitious manner. Any resemblance to actual persons, living or dead, or actual
events is purely coincidental.

IN SEARCH OF ANCIENT

Atlantis

by Phillip Gregoire

SCOTT COMPANY PUBLISHING
P.O. Box 9707 • Kalispell, MT 59904
Toll Free: 1-800-628-0212
Fax: 1-406-756-0098

Introduction

People have been looking for Atlantis since Plato said that it had sunk in the Atlantic ocean just west of Gibraltar. No trace of Atlantis had ever been found until two generals came upon some ancient buildings out in the desert during World War II.

Patton and Rommel were given some letters by the Elders of Atlantis, to help them find the last open entrance to Atlantis. Both generals would pass this information onto their relatives and that's when the Search for Ancient Atlantis begins.

Atlantis had to hollow out the center of the Earth, as a great flood was coming. A lottery was held, as only so many could be taken.

The traitors of Atlantis didn't like the lottery, because they weren't taken to the center of the Earth during the great flood. They have been looking for the last open entrance for many years. Then in 2018 they heard about the letters that were found.

The intruders of the Antichrist also found out about the letters and joined forces with the traitors to find this entrance and all the people from Atlantis. They wanted all their secrets and their souls.

Kent Patton and Petra Rommel found the letters together and were told by both generals what to do. They were told by the Elders to find Mark Doolittle and Jodie, who would join them in this great adventure.

This story was written by the author twenty-six years ago and just put into book form. He said, "A book not published isn't worth the paper it's printed on."

Found Then Lost Again

One of the world's legendary ancient mysteries is that of Atlantis. Plato said that this island sunk beneath the sea in the Atlantic, just west of Gibraltar. Many stories have been written about Atlantis and the people who lived there. Many have said that these people could read the stars and predict what was going to happen in the future.

These people had a special knowledge of the Earth's weather and they had learned how to control the Earth's gravitational field. They had developed machines to ride in that could hover above the ground and they could control their speed and direction. They were said to have laser beams that could be set for size and length and could cut through solid rock. It was also said that they had learned to control aging and that most of their people lived a lifespan of well over one thousand years.

After all this time and all the stories that were told, no trace of Atlantis or its people had ever been found until World War II. When in Africa, two generals had come across each other by some ancient buildings. Then all was lost again until 2018 when Patton's cousin Kent found some letters in Patton's library.

Regressing back to November, 1942, General George Patton had gone to North Africa to fight the Desert Fox, Rommel. One day General Patton went into the desert alone. Patton was one of those people who felt he had lived before in another time and that he had been to many places on the earth. Then and there, he felt he had been to this desert just out of Sardalas in Libya at a prior time, in a prior life. As he drove around in his Jeep, he saw some ancient buildings with pillars protruding from the sand. About that same time, he saw a German officer run out of one of the buildings and jump into a half-track vehicle. The German officer turned and looked back. Patton could see that it was Rommel. Rommel saluted Patton and drove off over the sand dunes into the night.

As Patton pulled up to the ancient buildings, he could see a very bright light coming from the entrance. He pulled both his pistols and went over to the entrance but no one was there. Patton could see that a metal door was built right into the solid rock. On the door was what seemed to be a picture and the numerals one through ten. He put his hand up to what appeared to be a scanner and a voice emanated from the door.

It said "Welcome Citizen of ATLANTIS. Here is a print out of this location." Patton took the printout and looked at the numeral printed on it, it was the number "3". He continued to read the document when he heard the voice from the door once again. It said that all the other numerals were now taken and that Rommel had possession of them. Patton was instructed to go to Rommel's home in Germany. Patton could hear tanks coming, so he ran out to his Jeep and took off for his front lines. The next day he showed the letter to his aide, but his aide couldn't read the letter, for he didn't know what language it was written in. Patton of course could read the letter. Just maybe he was thinking, I am from ancient Atlantis.

Patton told his aide to put the letter away as Rommel was again attacking his front line. After many battles with Rommel, Patton went back to Sardalas, but he couldn't find the old buildings again. The sands had shifted during the months since he had been there. He went back again and again, but it had vanished into the sands of the desert.

Patton was pulled out of Africa as he was needed back in France because the American troops were being pushed back by two big Panzer divisions. They were trying to break through and drive the Americans back into the sea. Patton soon came to their aid at the Battle of the Bulge and drove them back into Germany. The war was just about over as the Germans were in full retreat back to Berlin.

Patton looked at his field map of Germany as he stopped at the border. He wasn't too far from Rommel's hometown. He got into his Jeep and drove to Herrlingen and asked at the hotel where the Desert Fox lived. Patton went to Rommel's home and as he arrived at the front door it opened and a lady gave him a letter. She told him what Erwin had said, "Patton would come, give him this letter." Then the lady closed the door. Patton just stood there in shock. How did Rommel know that he would come? He must have been a citizen of Atlantis in the past just as he was.

Following the war, Patton learned what had happened to Field Marshal Erwin Rommel. Rommel had informed Hitler that it was futile for Germany to continue the war. Rommel was implicated in the plot to kill Hitler. Given two choices, Erwin Rommel took the latter, which was poison. George Patton knew all too well that it didn't do any good to tell your opinions to people of higher rank.

Patton was sitting in his office in Germany looking at the two letters that came from the ancient Atlantis buildings in Africa. He read and reread the letters and the notes that were written on the back of Rommel's letter, by Rommel. Patton just couldn't believe what the letters said. Deciding to discuss the letters with a good friend, Patton hopped into his Jeep and told his driver to go to his friend's house. But he never reached his destination; there was an accident and George Patton died of his injuries suffered in the crash. He was buried in a Third Army cemetery at Luxembourg with his men. His personal papers and books were sent back to his home and placed in his library. The two letters were put into one of the books.

There they sat in Patton's library undiscovered until April 20, 2018, when Patton's cousin Kent was browsing through the library and stumbled upon the letters. He read them through along with what Patton had written on the back of one letter. Then he read what Rommel had written. He couldn't believe what he had read and when he showed the letters to other relatives staying in the home, they just started to laugh at him. Kent had told them that the letters were from Atlantis and that they told him to go to Germany.

"It's just another one of your jokes Kent," they told him. "There's nothing but a bunch of mixed up letters and some markings on the letters."

Kent couldn't get anyone to believe in the reality of the letters. Kent was just like General Patton, both loved to play jokes on their relatives.

It was hard for Kent to believe what he had read himself, how could he expect others to believe his statement that they were written in Atlantean hand script by people from Ancient Atlantis and that one of them was Patton.

On the back of the second letter, Rommel had written instructions to contact a certain relative and to inform them where to find the other letters. Prior to his death, Rommel had written notes in Atlantean hand script on the back of all the letters, telling Patton what to do in case he should die before they could meet to review all the letters. After Rommel had written the notes, he had a vision which revealed to him what was going to happen to him and Patton.

Kent Patton had the telephone number from the notes Rommel had written on the back of the letter just before he died. How could he know what the telephone number would be years into the future? Kent dialed the number to Rommel's home and it started to ring on the other end. It just kept ringing and Kent was just about ready to hang up when someone finally said, "Hello?" Kent asked to speak to Rommel's cousin Petra.

"Hold on, I'll see if I can find her, it might be a few minutes as I'm old and slow."

After about ten minutes went by, Petra said, "Can I help you?"

Kent told her why he had called and they both started to speak in Atlantean. Kent told her where to look for the books. He waited on the phone for a long time and wondered why it was taking her so long. When she returned to the phone, she told Kent that one of the books had been sold, that she was only able to locate three letters and the other two were missing. Their conversation continued, in German, English, French and Atlantean.

Finally, they couldn't think of anything more to say and agreed that Kent should come to Germany as soon as possible.

Rommel had guaranteed that this trip would transpire. He had deposited over a million dollars in a Swiss bank account in the joint names of Kent Patton and Petra Rommel. This was one of the details written on the back of one of the letters. Now the adventure began, in search of ancient Atlantis and its people.

Date - April 20, 2018

How was it that Rommel would know the name of Patton's cousin or the name of his own cousin? What was it that prompted him to deposit money into a Swiss bank account? Who or what told him that Patton would go to his home in Germany? What led Rommel to put notes on all the letters pertaining to the locations of the seven entrances to the center of the earth where Atlantis could now be found? How did he know the details as to what was going to happen in the future?

Kent and Petra were both 25 years old and were born at the same time on the same day. They were like identical twins. Both had taken all the same subjects in school. They both could fly airplanes, helicopters and were experts in the martial arts.

Kent was just over six feet tall and weighed 190 pounds. He

had dark blue eyes, was a good-looking lad and had a military look about him like he just got out of boot camp. Many of his relatives said he looked a lot like General Patton did when he was young.

Kent told his family that Rommel had put money in a Swiss bank for him and Petra. He showed them his bank account and they couldn't believe their eyes.

"I'm going to Germany in the morning to meet with Petra Rommel and hunt for the ancient city of Atlantis," he explained. He told them that Rommel had written in the letters that the people from Atlantis had left letters that would help lead them to Atlantis. They just sat there in shock, unable to talk.

During his plane trip to Germany, Kent wondered what Petra looked like and whether he would know her at first sight. As he went through customs, Petra walked up to him and they knew each other instantly. They were communicating with each other, but no words were spoken. They both realized this at the same time and started to laugh together. They were communicating with their minds. This was to be their greatest ability, saving their lives on many occasions in the future during their search for the seven entrances to the center of the earth.

Following their arrival at Petra's home, they talked for hours about their respective homes and one another's experiences and interests in life. They were two separate people, but they thought as one in all things.

Petra was just like Kent had visualized, a tall blue-eyed blond of German descent and a body to go with her good looks.

After a few days of sightseeing and rest, they sat down at

the table in Rommel's library and began to go over the letters they had in their possession. They had the letters numbered two through six; numbers one and seven were missing, the first and the last of the sequence. The young couple started with the second letter. Patton and Rommel had both written notes on the back of the letter, providing clues in case any of the other letters came up missing. Rommel knew that if letters number one and seven were not available, the codes for the locations of the seven entrances could never be broken. It was revealed that only one of the seven entrances would be in operation in the 21th century, due to the shifting of the earth's plates. Kent knew that these plates were moving in all directions from the book he read on plate tectonic theory.

Rommel had found the letter number two in Egypt. He had deciphered a drawing on the Sphinx, which indicated that a person had to look for an old building and an entrance at location 30.47° North and 31.00° East. Above the entrance an inscription would say, "Jehoram, King of Atlantis." Rommel found this entrance and the voice from the metal door instructed him to go to Sardalas. From there, he was instructed to go out into the desert towards Ghat on November 28, 1942, as that would be the only day on which the building and entrance would be visible above the sand. Rommel was successful in his search as he found the old building and the entrance. The voice from the metal door at entrance number three, as well as letter number three, informed Rommel what was going to happen and instructed him as to what he was to do in order that the last forty Atlantis citizens and their offspring would be able come home to the center of the Earth. That explained why Rommel waved at Patton.

Kent and Petra were selected in advance by the Elders of Atlantis to do the job. They were now the ones instructed to read all the letters they had, starting with number two, decipher all the clues and record them. All the letters began the same way.

Letter Number Two

To our God of the heavens who made everything. To the only true God who takes care of all the people in the Universe. The people of Atlantis give all their love and devotion to.

To the lost citizens of Atlantis

Our Elders have constructed seven entrances to the center of the Earth, our new home. As you know from our first meeting on the survival of our people, the surface of the Earth was going to be flooded. The magnetic fields of the poles were going to change. There would be 1,000-foot tidal waves over our island home and other parts of the Earth. The changes to the weather on the surface of the Earth would be so great that food would be hard to find. Where once it was warm now it would be cold; very few people would survive these conditions.

As you all know we only had time and material to build seven thermo units, as our time was growing short to get the job done. We also had to make seven entrances to our new home that we made in the center of the Earth. We had hollowed out the center of the Earth with our laser beams and the Elders had made an eternal light with the same abilities as the sun.

We had to construct a method to transport our people, but we could only make them big enough to hold forty people at one time. As you know names were drawn for each location and you had to travel there at your own risk.

Remember, some of our people turned against the Elders. They didn't like the lottery and thought they should go because they were better than the ones that were chosen. Those traitors will try to stop you and try to destroy the entrances. Their abilities have been taken away by the Elders. If they get in your way, use your abilities that we gave you to stop them. At each entrance we will have one thermo unit with a built-in laser beam. This beam can harden any material, melt it, or eliminate it.

The thermo unit can only take forty people on each trip to the center of the Earth. It will take three hours to make a round trip. This will take three months to get all our people to our new home, but it will still leave over 20,000 of our people on the face of the Earth. Time is running out. You must sign in at each location. Each location will scan your hand for identification and order of entry per the lottery selection.

All gates will be opened after the great flood for all survivors. Good luck to all citizens. Your friend and King, Jehoram.

Remember, the first are last and the last are first. The locations are both together because they are one. But the fourth is also first.

Kent and Petra wrote down the clues and then took out the

third letter. Would this be the letter to give information to the only entrance left in operation on the face of the Earth? Kent and Petra were reading the letter when they discovered the part regarding their abilities.

Letter Number Three

Don't forget your abilities. Use them to survive if you don't make it to our new home. You will have five extra abilities.

Ability One

Use your eyes to project laser beams of light to blind people for up to five minutes. You can't use these beams on any other citizens of Atlantis, just the traitors, so trust no one as each person you meet could be one of them.

Ability Two

Use the force field in your body to unlock and open doors, move walls and find hidden passageways just by touching them.

Ability Three

Use this ability to communicate with your mind, but remember it's only good for a distance of 100 miles. So it is necessary to stay close to your people because you might need help. If you want to talk any farther than that you will need a power belt.

If they're traitors from Atlantis you will be able recognize them with your mind.

Ability   Four

You have the ability and the power to disappear once each day for five minutes. Use this ability to your advantage.

Ability   Five

You have the ability to put a force field around you for two hours. Nothing can pass through this force field, not even water or air. After two hours your air supply will run out. You must break the force field at that time. If you pass out you will die. Only the one who knows your code can then save you and break your force field. Take your time to choose who you will give this secret code to. It could cost you your life if you are not careful.

Remember

The first is last and three and five are first. The map will tell you the truth. Use it.

They both wrote down all the clues. By this time they were very tired and they quit for the night. During the night, just a few hours before dawn, four people broke into the house and tried to find the letters in Rommel's library. Petra and Kent heard them come in. As they approached the library, they were attacked by the four intruders, each armed with a large knife. A full-scale fight started, but they were experts in hand-to-hand combat and after a few strategic moves, they disarmed the intruders and drove them off into the night. Following the fight, they were so keyed up they couldn't get back to sleep. These were not the traitors from Atlantis as their minds didn't recognize them. They were people who worked for the Antichrist. They both wondered why would these people attack them.

Letter Number Four

They took out the fourth letter and started to check the back of the letter for notes. At exactly the same moment, each realized that they hadn't checked the back of letter three for any notes.

"We can't make that mistake again Kent, I know we were both getting tired, we better get the coffee going," Petra observed. They checked the back of letter three, where Patton had written the instructions. He told them how to use the five new abilities they were given, the abilities that each and every Atlantis citizen possessed except for the traitors. They were told to practice the use of these abilities before moving to a secret location. It was clear that whoever had the missing letters was trying to kill them to obtain all the other letters. The two young people would need these abilities to survive the trip to the secret location.

Patton revealed in his notes that letter number four was the key to all the other letters and the location of each. What Patton revealed next left them in total amazement. In two weeks time, all the letters would be electronically changed forever. The letters would be worthless. It was critical that Kent and Petra write down all the clues from all the letters, which were in their possession and they must do it immediately or risk loss of the important information for all time. After a few days of practicing the five new abilities, each was ready to move to the new location.

Patton had also revealed in his notes that the traitors of Atlantis had lost the five abilities. However, these traitors were never to be underestimated. They were ruthless and were paid great sums of money for their destruction. As Kent and Petra looked out the window, they could see that they were being watched. There was no question of that; they were now on their own and had to figure out how to get to the new location. Each took time to memorize the clues, the location and the secret passageway identification number. They knew that the secret hideaway was the location of Atlantis prior to its sinking. There they would find one of the old buildings with an ancient library located in its interior that was still air locked. There were lamps in this library that the ancient Atlantis people had created which stayed illuminated forever as eternal lights. The lights had a chemical sealed inside the glass. As long as the lights remained sealed with the glass intact, they would burn forever.

This secret along with others, would be revealed to the two young people in letter number four. The letters number five and six would give other information and other clues. But first, they needed to reach 10°west and 35°north. It was the place Plato had written about many years earlier, just off Gibraltar. Patton in his notes repeatedly warned the two not to get over 100 miles from each other or their ability to communicate between themselves using their minds would be lost.

The people who were after Kent and Petra were traitors of Atlantis and these people had paid large sums of money to others on the Earth to assist them in destroying the people of Atlantis.

Kent and Petra knew from the two letters which they had already read, that diamonds and hidden treasures had been discovered in the Earth when the thermo units were built. They were seeking to locate the ten solid gold rings which were twelve feet thick and ran over a thousand miles each, all emanating from the same location. Patton indicated that all notes on the back of letter number three must be erased just as soon as those notes were committed to memory. That was the only way to protect the location of old Atlantis. Once they had reached the location, they could work on the remaining letters to discover the last entrance to the center of the Earth.

After their memorization of the notes and erasing all the notes, they sat down to mull over their escape plan. They devised a foolproof scheme. Petra would rent a plane to go shopping at Freiburg. She knew that they would tell the traitors and that she would be followed by them. When in the air she would tell the pilot to fly over the valley where an old German airfield use to be. When she was ready to jump, she would pull the wires off the radio and jump out of the airplane. In the meantime, Kent would walk over to the airport and ask to check out the rentals. When he found one filled up and ready go, he would walk around the building out of sight. He would then use his ability to disappear, take the airplane and fly over to pick up Petra at the old airport.

"O.K. Kent, let's put the plan to work," Petra said. "We better do it now."

Everything went according to plan and as Kent was taking off he could see the men running around by the office. On the ground the men were saying to call the boss Glenn and tell him someone took an airplane.

"He accused us of drinking on the job last week Bill. What do you think he's going to do when we tell him the plane took off but no one was in it? Let's just report the plane missing in the morning. Let the insurance handle it."

Petra was now in the airplane heading over to the old airport and was about ready to jump when the pilot was told to return to the airport.

"You just sit there young lady," the pilot told her. "I wouldn't want to have to shoot a young thing like you."

Before he could pull his gun out she used her eyes to temporary blind him. She pulled the wires off the radio and jumped out of the plane. Petra then talked to Kent with her mind, telling him to pick her up at the old airport.

When she got on the ground she could see another plane following the one she had jumped from. Kent was coming in for a landing when she saw the other two planes turn back towards the airport.

Petra ran for the plane and when she got in she told Kent, "We better get out of here, we've got two planes after us."

He took off and kept the plane heading into the sun just above the tree line. The other pilots didn't even see them as they were only looking for the girl who had jumped. Soon Kent and

Petra were out of sight of the other planes and heading for the sunken city. They both had used their abilities to get out of town and away from the traitors.

One of the notes in the letters told him to fly to Geneva to pick up a pilot that Patton had recommended, Mark Doolittle. They came in for a landing at the airport and when they stopped, Mark jumped right in. He was actually one of the lost citizens of Atlantis with all the same special abilities and would be one of the last forty people going to Atlantis.

"I'll take over as you two need to get some rest," Mark assured them. "I know where to go as the Elders have been talking to me."

Now the plan was merely to jump out of the plane once it reached the 10°W and 35°N destination. They could use their fifth ability and place a force field around them. Nothing could penetrate this force field, not even water or air. The two would be safe to dive down to the old library in ancient Atlantis.

Date - April 29, 2018

After many hours in the air, the plane reached the destination. Kent and Petra hooked up their leads and jumped clear of the plane. The parachutes opened and they came down together into the water. They used their skills to dive down under the water so they could find a hidden passageway that took them into the ancient library that was airtight. Petra and Kent used each other's code to break the force fields around them and again were back to normal.

Mark turned the plane around and headed for Casablanca. When he landed the airplane he used his fourth ability to disappear. He got out of the plane, walked to the control tower and couldn't be seen. Traitors swarmed all over the plane, searching for the pilot. No one and nothing else could be found on the plane. The escape was perfect.

Just as the notes had stated, they had found the entrances. The lamps were still lit. They found some rooms full of ancient books and pottery. All the rooms were still air locked, even after all these years. Both of the young people were very tired and were soon fast asleep, safe from the traitors. The next day, Kent and Petra were very eager to go through the rest of the letters. Time was getting short, soon the letters would be erased. After eating some food they took out letter number four again.

The letter began by telling of the eternal lights and the secret of making them. It described the secret of using gravity, so no fuel was needed to move a vehicle. There was the ability to slow down aging, so that the average life span was well over 1,000 years. There wasn't any sickness. Every one of the major illnesses had been conquered. The Elders and the King had the ability to look into the future, but the letter didn't say how far into the future or the secret on how to do this. Letter four was giving out lots of information that would take time to think out. The clue to letter one and seven and the location of each letter was given.

"Four is first and it's last just like one and seven. It's the same when all the clues are added up and this is the location of one when you add nothing to it. It's where the dogs rock. Now the location of seven is the first and it's one added to the location of one. Now you have a date with location seven, but only the west changes. Now four is one more than old Atlantis and they both cross underwater."

Rommel had worked out the location of number one entrance to the center of the Earth. The clues meant that one and seven are eight. Because four was first and it was last, it meant that four and four were eight. That's the location of one when nothing is added to it. Therefore, if you add nothing to eight, it's 80 and that's where the Dog Rock is just off Cuba at 24°N.

The location of One is at 80°W and 24°N

The location of letter seven per the clues was to add one to the location of letter one, but only the west changes. So, one added to the west location is 180°W and 24°N, which puts it on the date line according to these instructions.

Kent and Petra were now finding the clues more rapidly and the locations were coming to them more easily. Now four is one more than old Atlantis and they both cross underwater. Looking at the map, they could see that old Atlantis was at 35°N and when adding one, you now have 36°N and 4°W, the location of letter four, at the coordinates which cross underwater.

Letter Number Five

Now the two took out the fifth letter. This letter gave out a list of the other 38 people that they were going to take with them to the center of the Earth. The pilot Mark, who had taken them to their jump site over old Atlantis was on the list. He was a relative of Jimmy Doolittle, the famous World War II pilot.

The fifth letter had also stated that the people on the list would all help Kent and Petra at various times during the search for the right entrance. The clues from the fifth letter seemed to come easy for them. To find this place one had to be in the sun in this city.

Look for the sun and its capital and that would be the fifth location. Tokyo, Japan was this city and its location was 35.42°N and 139.46°E.

Letter   Number   Six

The sixth and last letter was now in front of them. Soon their great adventure would begin with the other 38 people of old Atlantis. This letter was short and to the point. There was only one entrance to the center of the Earth which was still in operation. The Elders had decided to bring forty relatives each of the last forty Atlantis citizens home. The location had to be found within three months as it had the only thermo unit that was still working. Once they found the location they needed to make six more thermo units and place them into the other entrance locations to start moving all the forty Atlantis people and their forty relatives to the center of the Earth.

The letter continued, "The date and time of this event is being set by the Rapture of the Christians who believe in Jesus Christ. A funny thing will happen to our people on the Earth after the

Rapture; they will then believe that Jesus Christ is the Son of our God and that he has a brother called The Holy Spirit, who is God's brother. We must be ready for this Rapture or all the remaining citizens of Atlantis seeking to reach their destination will die on the surface of the Earth. After the Rapture we will have but three and a half years to find everyone and move them to our new home. We all know that time goes by faster than we have made time for doing all the things we planned to do.

"A great star named Wormwood is going to pass so close to the Earth that all life might be burned up from the heat and it will make all the water bitter to drink. Some rich people will escape in space ships but only a very few. No one on the Earth has the knowledge of the approaching star other then you and the Elders.

"The traitors of Atlantis and the intruders of the Antichrist are going to try stop these last forty Atlanteans from going home. The traitors wanted to destroy these remaining people because they want all the secrets and all the treasures for themselves. The intruders just want to put their mark on our people so that they can make them part of their great religious system and take their living souls for this Antichrist. We will be looking into this to let you know what to do."

The letter then gave the clues to the final location. A nation of water with a king and queen and a bridge that falls down. That had to be London, England. They now had all seven locations of the entrances.

The Last Note From Atlantis

Kent and Petra were told to look for a wall in the library, which they could move with their minds. Behind this wall would be the Teleporting room. Petra found the entrance and used her mind to move the wall. Inside this room was a large machine, the Teleport. It had a large door on the front of it, which she opened to discover forty belts that she took out. One super capsule was programmed into the machine; it could be used over and over.

They were told to close the door and send it back. It would be used again in the future.

The Elders had made it to send power belts and other equipment to the last forty citizens. These belts would give them better abilities and a lot better chance of making it to the new Atlantis.

The directions on how to use the belts was with each one. Each was to be coded by the individual who put them on, so no one else could use them. The power belt had special glasses attached to it, which a person could use to control the intensity of the light beams from his number one ability. The belt also had the power to use and control satellites. That made it possible for ability number three, mind communication, to be utilized just about everywhere on the Earth. The 100-mile limitation was virtually eliminated with the use of the satellites with the power belt, except where electrical force fields were in existence.

The power belt contained an oxygen canister on it for manufacturing oxygen. This made it possible to remain underwater for indefinite periods of time when the force field ability was used. A visual projection power was also available with the belt. It was so real that someone could sit down at a computer and communicate with other computers and persons around the world to find any information needed.

Petra and Kent were instructed to get the power belts to the other 36 people on the list.

Then A Personal Note

"May our God of the Heavens who made everything, the one and only God that we give our love and devotion to protect you from harm. Good luck, from the people of Atlantis."

They took the belts and put them on the table in the library. They took all their notes and wrote down all seven locations of the entrances.

Location Library. 10°W and 35°N Underwater. Teleport from Atlantis.

Location One. 80°W and 24°N Just off Cuba by The Dog Rocks.

Location Two. 30.47°N and 31.00°E In Egypt.

Location Three. 25.59°N and 10.33°E By Sardalas.

Location Four. 36°N and 4°W In the Mediterranean.

Location Five. 35.42°N and 139.46°E Tokyo, Japan.

Location Six. 51.30°N and 0.07°W London, England.

Location Seven. 180°W and 24°N Pacific Ocean, International Date Line.

Now they must leave their secret hideaway and take a belt to each person on their list. The first two people to contact would be the pilot Mark, who flew them to old Atlantis, and his partner Jodie. What they didn't know then, was that they would utilize this place again and again to move from one location to another. They picked up the belts and headed for the surface. They each had given one another the codes to their power belts and force fields. As instructed, they left behind all the letters and notes in the old library and committed everything to memory. They could always return if they found it necessary. Each person on the list from the Elders would have to be found and given a power belt.

They put their belts on and Kent told Petra he was going to try to get hold of the pilot who flew them there.

"Mark Doolittle and Jodie, I know you both can hear me in your minds. You can't talk to me until you get a power belt, you're too far away, I'll explain when you get here. Get a helicopter by any means that you can and bring Jodie with you as she's staying at the same hotel. Pick us up where we jumped from the plane, Kent Patton over and out."

Petra asked, "Do you think it's going to work?"

"It better, since we're too far out to swim to land."

It was at least an hour before they could hear Mark coming in. When they got into the helicopter, they gave Mark and Jodie all the information they had and gave both of them a power belt. The four of them told each other their codes.

"That was really something to hear your voice in my mind, calling my name," Mark said. I was sitting in a bar and just about jumped out of my skin, I thought you were right next to me. Jodie was in the bar and also heard what was said in her mind. When I asked her to come, all she asked was when are we leaving."

"When you learn to use the power belt Mark and Jodie, you will be able to do the same thing." Kent explained. "We will all need help to find all the entrances and the other 36 people on the list. We will have to find the entrance that is still working. Petra has the list of all the locations in her head. We will need a special plane. Come to think of it, a seaplane will be our best bet because half of the locations are underwater. I got the list of the people in my pocket written down in the Atlantis secret code that only people with the power belt can read."

Mark Doolittle had been wandering the world after his wife had been killed in a plane crash in Alaska. He was a rugged looking 53-year-old man with brown eyes that seemed to look right through you. He was a bush pilot, she was a doctor, and they had both loved Alaska. He could never get himself to go back to Alaska again, it hurt too much to just think about it.

Here he was with some new friends and a beautiful woman that he was very attracted to. He hadn't even tried to date again since he lost his wife. Jodie seemed to remind him of the love he use to feel, as he could feel the interest she was showing him.

News Flash From Atlantis

"Our scholars have found ancient writings that were hidden in books that were saved from the library at Alexandria when it was burned. We have traced our ancestry back to one of the lost tribes of Israel who also believed in the one true God. We didn't know Jesus Christ when we went into the Earth to get away from the great flood. The Jewish people knew this man that lived among them and saw him hung on a cross by the Romans. Some believed that this man was the Son of God, some of the Jews didn't and are still waiting for their Lord to come back to lead them. Christians and Jews and all the other religions, what a mix that is. No wonder things are going to hell up there.

"Whatever you do up there, you don't ever want to take the mark of this Antichrist. Fight these people, alert your people to what he's up to.

"We are still looking into the writings from Alexandria and are finding so much information that it will take us and our computers a few years to go through it all.

"The flood was caused by the poles switching and the electrical fields pulling the great river of water down that was put there to help protect people from the rays of the sun. Before the flood, people of the Earth could live over 900 years. After the flood it went down to 125 years old according to their Bible.

"We are providing a list of the 36 Atlantis Citizens that must be found and given a power belt. They also must be given all the information needed to lead forty people home.

"They must be told about the Antichrist, that if they take

his mark they will lose their soul and they can't come home to Atlantis. Read each person's mind with your ability number three to find out who has the mark. The mark is invisible to the naked eye but not to the mind. If you find one with the mark, drive them off, for they now belong to him and are evil and are lost forever.

"The list will have some well-known people, choose from the list the ones you can trust. Use your mind to check them for the mark. Your life and soul will depend on the right choices. If you find a bad one, throw them out. Don't let them come back in.

"Mark and Jodie, you each will choose nine people from the list. You will give each one a power belt and check them out for the mark. If they're OK, teach them the proper use of the belt. They must also check all the people that they're going to bring home to Atlantis for the mark. Again let me say, throw them out when you find them. Kent and Petra you both will choose nine people, and must do the same thing as Mark and Jodie. Good luck, you're going to need it.

"Don't use their last name when you talk to them, as the intruders and the traitors are now picking up all our mind signals with their new equipment. Remember, no last names. Keep your conversations under 30 seconds or they will find your location.

"Use the secret code from the list when you talk to your people with the power belt."

THE LIST. M for Mark, J for Jodie, K for Kent and Clark. P for Petra and Lois.
M1. Johnny 141.   J1. John 1201.   K1. Emma 1191.

M2. Tom 282.   J2. Jeff 272.   K2. Van 242.

M3. Tom 333.   J3. Kevin 333.   K3. Megan 353.

M4. George 434.   J4. Kurt 4184.   K4. Nicolas 434.

M5. Mathew 5135.   J5. Will 5195.   K5. Sandra 525.

M6. Denzel 6236.   J6. Morgan 666.   K6. Meg 6186.

M7. Angelina 7107.   J7. Brad 7167.   K7. Jason 7197.

M8. Liam 8148.   J8. Bruce 8238.   K8. Forest 8238.

M9. Sean 939.   J9. Matt 949.   K9. Samuel 9109.

P1. Steve 1191.   P4. Bradley 434.   P7. Wesley 7197.

P2. William 2132   P5. Kevin 525.   P8. Dwayne 8108.

P3. Harrison 363.   P6. Al 6166.   P9. Diane 9119.

"It's about time we get this helicopter back in the air and back to Casablanca," Mark told them.

On the way there, Jodie explained that when they were making a movie down by the ocean, she'd seen a lot of old seaplanes out in a field. They were right next to a closed up airport that hadn't been used since the war.

"We had to rebuild two of them for the movie. The movie making is now over and the planes have been parked in one of the old buildings. We can work on them in the building to update both of them. They will need the best weapon systems, computers and fuel capsules sent from Atlantis."

Jodie was very excited because the Elders of Atlantis had talked to her, communicating with their minds. They told her to tell Kent and Petra to come back to the library in five days, as they would be sending everything they'd need up with the Teleport.

As they approached the coastline two other helicopters came up to greet them. Mark dove right between them into the fog. Doolittle could see that they were well-armed and said, "As soon as we can set this thing down on dry land grab the belts and use your fourth ability. We must get away from the helicopter as they're going to blow us to hell and back."

They had no more then just sat down when the two helicopters came in with their guns ablazing and the helicopter went up in flames. They had been lucky the fog bank hid them till they could land. The four crouched behind some logs on the beach as they would soon become visible again.

After the helicopters touched down, men jumped out and ran all around the burning wreck, yelling, "No one got out of that alive. Not a single person got out of that helicopter when it landed. Let's get out of here and report back to the Antichrist's headquarters that we got them, they're all dead. Our reward will be great, two months at any resort that we want to go to!"

"Now that they think we're dead we can move around right under their noses."

Soon the team from Atlantis was heading for the old airport Jodie had told them about.   When they got there, they put all their belts in the seaplane.

"Let's go downtown and get something to eat. They don't know that Mark and Jodie are on our team, so we will use their debit cards."

Kent had received a mind communication from Atlantis telling him to destroy any cards or identification that he or Petra had. When they got back to the sunken library they would have new and untraceable identification waiting for them.

"Enjoy your dinner and in five days you must return to the library."

They spent most of their time working on the planes and storing needed provisions. They were about out of money on both cards and still needed fuel for the two planes. There was only enough fuel in one plane to get out to the library, but not enough to get back. They were told by the Elders to fly out as they had sent fuel capsules up from Atlantis. Soon it was time to take off in the old seaplane. They all took turns flying the "Old Tub One", their call sign for the seaplanes. When they got over the library, Mark took over and landed the plane, then Kent and Petra dove down to the library.

They went right to the room where the Teleport was hidden. There on the information center on the Teleport was a list of what was sent. They had included a laser with instructions on how to cut a tunnel through the earth right under the hanger. They then could use the power sled to transport all the guns, ammunition and rockets right to the hanger. They had also sent fuel capsules to make fuel out of water. Just drop one in a 500-gallon tank of water and in two minutes you had fuel. There was new paint that would absorb all radar signals. The stealth color would render the planes hard to see in the air, although the enemy would still be able to hear them. There was also a packet with new IDs for Kent and Petra, and four boxes of money to buy food for all the people and to pay the guards who would keep them safe from the intruders.

Kent talked with his mind to the two up in the plane, telling them what was sent and that they would bring up portable pumps and fuel capsules. It took some time to hookup the pumps to the tanks to be filled.

"Once the plane's fuel tanks are full of water, drop in the fuel capsules, go back to the hanger and wait for us."

Mark took off for the hanger and flew low to keep off the radar alert system. The old seaplanes could land either on land or in the water. They were just pulling up to the door after landing, when a truck with armed guards came up next to them. They were told to get out of the plane with their hands up in the air.

One of the guards recognized Jodie and told the other guards it was OK, that she was making a movie about the war. He apologized for pulling the guns on them and explained someone had called in and told them the old seaplane had been stolen right out of the hanger.

"Thank you for checking on the plane, but we're still working on the movie for at least two more months," Jodie improvised. "We might need some extras in the future and the pay is good, that's if you would be interested."

The guard told her, "You bet, you can call us any time you need us."

Jodie told them they would be gone at times and would like someone to keep people away from the hanger. The guards assured her they'd keep it safe and left, thinking to themselves they were going to be stars.

Kent had used the laser to cut a tunnel to the hanger and they put everything on the power sled. They were at the hanger before the plane landed and had the sled unloaded. They had overheard

Jodie's conversation with the guards, and Kent thought, "That Jodie sure is smart, she has the police pulling guard duty for us."

Petra pushed the button and the door opened to the hanger. Mark pulled the plane in and shut the two engines down just as the hanger door closed. They were now safe from the intruders and the traitors.

On one end of the hanger there were living quarters for at least forty people. They had four deep freezers and large walk-in pantries filled with everything you could think of. They could stay here for over a year and not run out of food. The girls started to make supper while the guys began to check out what Atlantis had sent them.

"Hey guys, the supper is ready. Let's eat so we can talk about what we're going to be doing for the next few days."

They talked well into the night about the things they'd received from Atlantis. Petra had noticed the looks and the kidding that were going on between Mark and Jodie. They wanted to know about the library and what they had found there.

"It's just an old library and bunch of old books, there really isn't that much to see. Why don't you two take the power sled to the library and have a look for yourself?" Before Kent could say another word, they were in the sled heading for the library. "Boy, what did I say that made them take off so fast?" Kent asked.

"I think I'm going to take a shower and head for bed since all the people with any common sense have left the hanger, Petra announced. Kent watched her walk away as he wondered what the hell she meant by that statement. The Elders talked to Kent with their minds and told him not to swear.

"Just take a shower and go to bed, common sense will come hand in hand to you tomorrow." Kent took a shower and as he climbed into bed, he was thinking, "That's just what I need, another stupid riddle. Hand in hand, common sense coming to me, sure it will just walk right up to me to hand in hand."

When he got up the next morning, Kent could smell the bacon and the hot coffee.

"It's about time you got up, I was just about ready to come and wake you up. Please sit down and eat as we all have a lot of work to do today," Petra told him.

"You better wake up Mark and Jodie so they can help us."

"That would be hard to do as they haven't come back from the library."

"You mean they've been gone all night?" Kent asked.

Just then Petra could hear the power sled coming back from the library. When the sled pulled up into the hanger, Mark and Jodie jumped out and walked up to Kent hand in hand with big smiles on their faces.

"Hope we're in time for breakfast. We were up all night talking about what we had to do today," they both chimed.

"I bet you two were up all night messing around. Kent, didn't the Elders talk to you about common sense that you were going to find when they walked up to you?" Petra asked.

"I hate this place, everyone can read your mind."

"So don't you get any ideas Kent, I'll know just what you're thinking before you think it. Let's eat."

While they were eating, Kent was looking at some notes from Atlantis. He took out the packet with the new identifications for him and Petra and started to laugh. "I'm now Superman. I am now Clark Kent and you're Lois Lane, Petra."

"Come to think about it, we got new names, so what's your last name, 'Miss Jodie'?"

"Kent, it's not proper to ask questions like you do!" Petra said. "Jodie is our friend and the Elders from Atlantis have chosen her to help us, just like they chose you, so be nice. If she wants to tell us her last name or just be Jodie, that's up to her, and another thing, never ask a woman her age."

"I wasn't going to do that," Kent claimed.

"You were thinking of asking her, don't forget Kent I can read your mind."

"Before I came to Casablanca, I had people following me everywhere I went," Jodie said. "One night they broke into my home and pulled me right out of bed. One of the kidnappers said, 'Don't hurt her, we will get a nice ransom for her.'

"My bodyguard had heard them come in and he attacked them, setting my arm free from their grasp and then he pulled the mask off one of them. 'Run Jodie, run,' he yelled. I ran to the neighbors and called the police and when they went into my home they found my bodyguard dead. They had left a note saying, 'You have seen one of us, if you identify him, you are dead.' We went to the police station to look at photos, I identified the man, and that's when I was told about the note. That's why I'm here, 'incognito.'"

"I'm sorry Jodie, I'll try to use the common sense in the future that the Elders just gave me this morning," Kent said.

After they finished eating, Mark said that he should be in

charge of mounting all the guns and rockets.

"I worked for Boeing and know the proper way to mount the guns and in the right locations. We don't want to shoot a wing off, as we will have to train all the people on the proper use of the weapons when we take them back to the entrances to Atlantis. Jodie and Petra can fill the gas tanks with water and put a fuel capsule in each tank. We have two 500-gallon tanks on each plane and the gas valves must be set to draw both tanks down at the same time, I will show them how to set the valves. We also have to mount two pumps on each plane to fill the tanks when we're sitting in the water. The girls must put all the fuel capsules in the cabinet by the tanks and keep it locked, as we will be picking up a lot of people. We might pick up an Intruder by mistake as we can't read their minds. If we lose the fuel capsules we will be rowing the planes back to our base. We already have everything else that we need on the plane.

"Jodie, when you're done with the tanks you can help load all the ammunition. Kent, you and Petra can get the paint guns out and get ready to coat the planes. It's a special colored paint that spreads all by itself. Just spray the top of the plane and it will cover the whole plane from top to bottom. We should be done by tonight. Tomorrow we can start hunting for the seven entrances and the one that is still open to the center of the earth."

They were all done with the plane by five. They put two big pizzas in the oven and took off for their own living quarters to take a shower. They were soon back eating the pizzas and talking about which location to go to first.

Kent said, "I'm not going to run all around the world looking for it when it's right here, just offshore in the Mediterranean Sea. I once read a book about a man that left his farm, wife and kids to look for gold all over the world. Ten years went by with no word from him. His wife thought that he had been killed, so she remarried. Her new husband was killed in a car accident and again she was left all alone. She was broke and the bank was going to take the farm away because they didn't want to loan her any more money.

"After twenty years he came home and saw his wife walking up the hill in the back yard. He called to her and she came running to him, hugging and kissing him. 'I'm sorry I left you, the gold fever got to me and I kept thinking I would find it over the next hill. I'm broke, never found enough to buy a ticket to come home till now. What were you doing going up the hill with a shovel?'

"'I need to dig a root house to store food for the winter, if the bank gives me another loan.'

"'Let me dig it for you honey, I'm good at digging, been doing it for the last twenty years.'

"'I'll go fix a nice supper for us, I'm so glad you're back, we have a lot to talk about.'

"He was happy to be home and his wife still loved him. The shovel dug into the hill again and again and he soon had a nice tunnel going deep under the hill. There right in front of him were gold nuggets all over in the dirt. It turned out to be the biggest gold mine in the state. He should have stayed right at home, twenty years wasted and nothing to show for it," Kent finished up. "I'm not going too far from here, we're going to location 36° N and 4° W first."

"You could be right Kent," Mark said. "We've got to start somewhere and I liked your story. It had a good ending, maybe ours will have a good ending too. Tomorrow we will find out."

In the morning after they ate, Kent gave Mark a GPS indicator to put at the last open entrance to Atlantis.

"Petra, you will fly the old tub, Mark and Jodie can dive down and if it's the last open entrance, just talk to me with your minds. I'll use the laser to cut a path right to the   entrance. I will come with the sled and tools to bring the thermo unit back to the hanger. Petra, bring the two guards that are on guard duty into the plane and have them run the machine guns, tell them they are now part of the movie."

They took off for the entrance 36°N and 4°W and were soon coming in for a landing. Mark and Jodie were ready to go and jumped into the water, then dove down to the entrance. They had to open an air lock door and once inside, close it and wait for the water to be pumped out. Then they opened the next door to find a large airtight room.

There it was, the large thermo unit.

They talked to Kent and told him he was right, the entrance was open. Kent turned on the laser. Petra told them to get back to the plane because a boat was approaching the seaplane at high speed. Petra had the engines revved up and ready to go when they climbed in. A plane was coming in fast from the north and was locking in their firing system when Petra sent a rocket in their direction. Mark and Jodie and the two guards started firing the machine guns at the boat as their old plane took off. They could see the plane burst into flames and fall into the sea. They were just above the boat and could see the rockets getting ready to launch at them. The paint had done its job and the radar guiding systems for the rockets couldn't see the plane. They were soon out of sight and heading for the hanger. The two guards were still talking and were all excited when they landed at the field. When the plane came up to the hanger, they jumped out and told the other two guards at the gate what had happened.

"It was so real, a plane shot down in flames and us shooting at this boat and bullets hitting our plane all around us. Jodie said that they would need us again in the near future and we would be paid good money for our roles in the film and for standing guard."

Once the tunnel was cut out by the laser, Kent took the sled down to the entrance. He removed the bolts from the thermo unit and hooked the cable from the sled to it. After lowering the loading ramp, he pulled the heavy thermo unit up onto the sled. He was soon heading back to the hanger but progress was slow because of the weight. Petra was getting worried as over two hours had gone by. Mind communication in the laser built tunnels didn't work due to a force field produced when they were made.

Standing by the new tunnel to listen for the sled returning, Petra told the others, "We better go back and check on Kent, he could be hurt or in trouble. I'll get the plane ready, we might need those two guards again."

"Hold on Petra, I think I can hear the sled coming back. It must be really moving slow because it's not making much noise."

It was another hour before the sled came out of the tunnel.

"Boy, are we glad to see you," Petra said. "We thought for sure that you had been hurt."

She put her arms around Kent and gave him a big kiss, and his face turned beet red. Everyone was laughing then but Kent.

"What took you so long to come back to the hanger?"

"This thermo unit weight was almost too much for the sled," he replied.

"Tomorrow Mark and Jodie will take the sled back to the library and send this unit back to Atlantis. They will build us six more thermo units using this one as a pattern. The paper work for the original thermo unit was lost during the great flood, so it was good that we found this one still working. Once you send the thermo unit to Atlantis by using the Teleport come right back as they want us to start picking up the people on the list.

"They want the first group you bring back to be placed in the two tunnels that were cut from the library to the hanger and down to the first location where the thermo unit was found. There are large living quarters in the library and at that location 36°N and 4°W."

The Elders told them all to start practicing using Kent and Petra's new IDs because they would be checked when they travel around the world. Kent and Petra were history. They were now Clark Kent and Lois Lane, reporters from Morocco News in Casablanca.

The next day Clark and Lois got the two planes ready to go while Mark and Jodie took the sled down to the library. Things were just starting to go right when they heard someone banging on the hanger door. It was the four guards from the gate wanting their money.

"We want to see Jodie about our money for standing guard and for our role we played in the movie."

"Come right over to the office door and we will sit down and talk about how much you think your time is worth."

The four guards went into the office and sat down. Clark and Lois came into the office with a sack full of money that had been filled from the one box. Jodie had filled 48 sacks with $40,000 in each sack.

"We want to see Jodie, who are you?"

"We are Clark Kent and Lois Lane, we are in the movie with you. Jodie said that we will need four of you to go with us today, we will need two men in each plane. You will be gone for at least two days each time we need you. You must find four good men to take over your guard duty when you're gone to keep crooks out of the hanger."

"We all have brothers that want to work for the movie company if the pay is good. They are all past military, well trained and know what they're doing and they hate these intruders who are trying to take over everything in Casablanca."

"How much do you want to do the job for us?"

"We think we're worth $2,000 each every month, as more people are checking around for these people from Atlantis."

"Jodie thinks you're worth a lot more than that because you can be trusted to protect us and the hanger from these intruders or anyone else that comes around. Here's a bag with $40,000 dollars for each month, that's $5,000 per man. If that's OK, take the bag and get your brothers back here as we will need you four to fly out with us this afternoon."

They picked up the bag and took off for the gate.

"Didn't I tell you that this Jodie was OK? You two stay by the gate, we will go get all our brothers and take this money to our wives, who have been telling us we will never get paid. And just think, we will be on the plane with Superman, as we all know Clark Kent is Superman."

Mark and Jodie came back to the hanger from the library and Clark told them about the guards. "I'm glad that I got the money ready and told you what to do."

"I can hear the guards coming to the office. Let's open the hanger doors and take the planes out on the runway. Put two guards in each plane to run the guns. Mark, you and Jodie will pick up your people at Geneva. Be sure to check them out as requested by the Elders. You can only bring forty people, that's our limit to bring back to Atlantis. The rest will be in God's hands and the Rapture if they're Christians.

"Petra, I mean Lois, and I will go to Herrlinger, Germany to bring her people back. I know it's going to be hard to choose which ones you will take, but at least we can save forty people from the intruders. It's a good thing that we can land in the water to refill our gas tanks as we will have to refill at least two times. It's just over 1400 hundred miles and we will spend just one day to load the plane with your people. So let's get the planes in the air."

Both planes took off since they were both heading in the same direction. The first stop was in the Mediterranean to fill up with water, and this stop went by with no one seeing them sitting in the water. They had just landed on their second stop for fuel when they were spotted by a fishing boat. The fishing boat had a large radio antenna and with a radar system built right into it. They were soon sending a report back to the local air base, about two planes landing just offshore. The report came right over their special scanner that Mark had installed in both planes.

"Keep your radar on Mark and let us know how much time we've got to fill up our tanks before those planes come at us."

The pumps were turning at full capacity and only had the tanks half full.

"That's it," Mark said. "Put the fuel capsules in the tanks and let's get out of here. The planes from the base are in the air and heading towards us."

Just then the fishing boat started up its powerful engines and came racing for them.

"Man the guns men, Lois and Jodie get ready to fire your rockets when you lock in on the planes."

The two old seaplanes turned right at the fishing boat and began firing as they got up speed to take off. Everyone on the boat was ducking for cover as the two guards on both planes were really laying down the lead. The two planes just missed the boat by a few feet when the crew on the boat turned their missiles at the planes, but again their radar couldn't lock in. This time they didn't have to fire the rockets, since the planes from the base hadn't locked in on them. The guards were told not to fire on the planes as they flew by them.

"We could have hit them with rocks, we could have shot

them both down," one of the guards said.

"How come?" one of the guards asked.

"We are invisible and don't want them to know we are here."

"We are in our stealth mode men, they can't see us when we're in the air. Boy this movie is really something, Superman, stealth mode, using water for gas and bullets that can't hurt us but can make holes right next to us on the plane and we get good pay for doing this."

The scanner was on and they could hear the pilots getting after the crew on the boat.

"I think you guys have been seeing things, there isn't a plane within a hundred miles of here."

"They shot us full of holes and took off, but once in the air they just disappeared."

"I think we better report this back to headquarters. This might be the people that they have been looking for."

"That was close Mark, too darn close," Clark said. "We can make it to Lake Geneva where you have a hanger at the edge of the water. While you round up your people, Lois and I will head for Germany to get her people. Be sure that everyone is cleared and also have them bring all their cell phones. Take all the cell phones away from them and put them into the lockers, no one is to use them until they're back in the two underground tunnels. They can't bring anything with them, and I mean nothing. Have the two guards search each person. We want it to look like they were taken by the intruders or the traitors. We should be back here tomorrow at this time, so be ready to go as they will be looking for us."

Once the tanks were full Clark and Lois took off for Germany. Clark could hear the Elders talking to him and all the people from Atlantis.

"The Rapture has happened."

"Millions of Christian people have just vanished from the Earth, maybe billions are gone with out a trace. Cars crashing into each other, with people still in the cars but the driver in one car was gone. Just what he was wearing was left in the car, shoes, hat, rings, watch, false teeth and even his knee parts he had replaced. Planes that were full are now half empty, both pilots gone and a bush pilot that was on the one plane had to land it. Other planes just going down, what a mess all around the world."

Date - October 23, 2018

"The President of Israel has told the Prime Minister to send out two witnesses and 144,000 male Christian workers from Israel to put the seal of God on the foreheads of all who believe that Jesus is the Son of God. This is the seal that will protect us from the plagues that will be coming on the face of the Earth. We are all Jews from the past and we will accept Jesus Christ as our God because he is the Son of our God.

"When you come across these people from Israel, let them put the seal on your forehead, for you will then belong to Jesus. It will take the Two Witnesses and 144,000 Christian workers a little over 1,260 days to put the seal of God on all the people who believe that Jesus is the Son of God. No one can stop them from going around the world for the days given to them by Jesus to bring salvation to the ones who believe in him. Those days will end when the Antichrist takes over.

That future date is Sat. Oct. 2021

"We will know more in the future; the Elders will let everyone know what is going on."

The next news story coming out of Israel over the radio and TV stations was that this Antichrist signed a seven-year treaty with Israel guaranteeing them safety from being attacked by other nations. He also gave them permission to rebuild their temple right on the Temple Mount, so they can again pray to their one true God Jehovah. He is their friend and would protect them at least until the Jewish temple is completed.

Clark and Lois, better known as Kent and Petra, were just a few miles from Herrlinger airport.

"Let's put down in the Blau River, Clark. I'll go into town and rent a bus and bring back forty of my relatives."

It was just starting to get dark as she got out of the plane.

"I'll be back at first light, if things should change and you can't stay here. Just talk to me with your mind and we will come to where you are."

Petra walked off into the night and Kent didn't like her going off by herself, but she was right, they just might find them sitting here in the dark. They could have heard them land and were now out searching for the plane. Clark told the guards to be on the lookout for anyone trying to find them.

"I'll be filling the tanks and looking for another place to land if they find us."

Things went real well through the night as it was cloudy and remained quite dark. The guards could see men with lights looking all over the shore and boats going up and down the Blau with their spotlights on, but none came towards the plane.

It was just starting to get light when Petra came flying down the road next to the Blau with at least ten police cars right on her butt with lights flashing and sirens on.

"Get ready men, we need to take out those police cars, every darn one of them before we can get the people off the bus onto the plane."

The two guards on their plane were the ones that were in their first firefight. Their guns were taking out the lead cars one after another. The other police cars were shooting at the bus and the plane. Bullets hit the plane all around them and one bullet took the fuel line right off the fuel tank.

"Keep shooting men, we've got to take out those cars and stop the fuel leak or we're all going to go up in flames."

One of the guards told Clark, "Take over my gun. I'll fix the fuel line as I'm a good plumber by trade when I'm not standing guard." Clark jumped right behind the gun and soon they had all the police cars out of commission as the bus pulled up next to the Blau.

He took the plane up onto the riverbank when the bus door opened.

Petra said, "We've got some wounded people on the bus that will need to be helped onto the plane."

Clark told the one guard to help the wounded get on the plane and the other guard to get the gas line fixed or the only place they would be going is up in flames. They soon had all the people on the plane.

"Kent," you could hear the fear in her voice. "We've got boats coming at us on both sides and the early warning system has two planes and a helicopter closing fast."

"I think we're all dead Petra, we can't take off without that gas line being fixed."

"We're not dead yet, the gas line is fixed so let's get out of here. I told you I was a good plumber, I'm the best plumber in Casablanca, people call me from all over the country to fix their leaks and I'm not even going to charge you for fixing the line."

"Please, please get behind the gun and see if you can help us get out of here," Lois said.

Clark turned the plane onto the road from the shore and took off down the road to get up enough speed to take off. Once in the air they would be flying right over the airport. The two guards shot at the boats and one went up in flames. The helicopter was right behind them, but the two guards took it out and it also went up in flames.

Petra locked in on the two planes and fired the missiles as Clark got the old tub into the air. Over the scanner they could hear the two pilots talking who were starting to lock in on them.

"They're gone off the screen, the screen is now blank, our radar must have gone out."

"Look out," was the last thing they heard. Just then the sky lit up as the two planes blew up and went down in flames right onto the other's still on the runway. Things were still blowing up at the airport when Clark turned for Lake Geneva.

It didn't take too long to get back to Geneva. Clark was coming in for a landing when Mark spoke to him.

"Don't land Clark, they are waiting for you. Someone on your plane used a cell phone to tip them off that you will be coming here to land by my dock. I've got a bus load of people waiting to get on the plane, but I can't ask Jodie to come to where we are and I can't go to the dock where she is."

"I'll get back to you Mark, I think I know who it is."

The guards were the only ones that weren't checked for cell phones. Clark called the guard over who fixed the fuel line and asked him what his name was.

"It's Mike O' Riley Sir, O' Riley the plumber from Casablanca."

"You know this is just a movie don't you Mike?"

"You bet Mr. Kent, it's just a movie."

"I want you to go over to the other guard and open the door and throw him out of the plane, right now."

Mike went over and opened the door, then they could hear the other guard screaming all the way down to the water.

"Don't worry Mike, your friend landed in a net. We will pick him up when we come back on our next trip. See that man who's in uniform Mike? Have him man the other gun. We're going to need him, he's been well-trained and is ready for action."

"Mark and Jodie, I'm going to clear a path for Mark to drive right up to the old tub. Get your missiles ready to go Jodie, and have your two guards ready to fire as soon I tell you to come out."

Clark turned towards the air base.

"Let's take out the planes on the ground before they can get into the air Lois. How many missiles do you have left?"

"Just four and they're all armed and ready to go."

"Fire two into the planes on the runway, we might need the other two as they could come from another airport before we can get out of here. Those two will make a mess of things and I'll tell the gunners to shoot at anything that moves."

They were soon over the air base where there were six planes armed and ready to go. The two missiles hit home while the guns were hitting fuel tanks and four helicopters that were also armed and ready. Everything went up in flames.

"We never would have had a chance if we had landed."

Clark turned the plane headed for Mark.

"Mark I can see the bus, I'll take out everything in front of you, get to the plane and I will try to cover you until everyone's aboard."

Clark made a complete circle of the dock and saw two boats coming towards the dock.

"We're ready to go Clark, give us some fire cover, we're coming out."

"Jodie, we got four planes coming in from the west. We'll fire on the two lead planes, the other two are up to you."

Lois fired her last two missiles as Clark turned toward the two boats. Both missiles hit home just as gunners on their plane destroyed the boats.

One of Jodie's missiles misfired and one plane got through. It was just about ready to fire on them when she got their plane into the air. She turned and fired another missile that hit home. There were burning planes falling out of the sky.

"Let's get out of here, there are a lot of planes coming in with heat sensing equipment on board. The scanner is picking up the pilot's conversations saying to fire missile when they pick up any indication of heat, that they're bound to hit something. We better shoot off the special flares that float down with the parachutes that are attached to them. They will think for sure that they hit something."

The missiles came at the flares and blew them up and they went down on fire.

"We got some of them for sure, radio back to the base and tell them we saw two go down on our radar scanner."

Both old tubs were heading back to the hangers with everyone safe aboard. They made one landing out in the Mediterranean to refuel and after a few hours were coming in for a landing at the hanger. As they pulled up next to the hanger door, the guards came running up to the planes.

"You better get unloaded as fast as you can, we had these intruders demanding to see what's inside these hangers. They said they would be back in force and if we got in the way we would be arrested and our heads would be cut off. I think they mean it, as that has been going on all over the world. We just quit and want more money so we can go up into the hills to hide."

"We have plenty of room for you and your families right here, as we have built underground shelters deep into the Earth. Go and get your wife and kids right now and come back here after the intruders leave."

One of the guards asked, "Where is my brother?"

"He jumped out of the plane into a net when we were over Lake Geneva," Mike said.

"Why did he do that?" Mitch asked.

"Your brother is going to protect the dock at the lake and tell us if it's OK when we come back next week. Mitch, come with me," Clark said. "We have a very special job for you and need your help as we have found diamonds, old coins and gold. We need someone we can trust to get it all boxed up for us."

"I'm the right man for that job Clark, as I work at the local bank, just lead the way."

"Mitch, can I use your cell phone my battery is dead?"

"You bet, here's mine."

"Thanks."

"Let's unload these planes and get the people into tunnels heading for the two underground chambers. Mark, take your people and the ones that are hurt down to the library on the sled. I almost forgot, take Mitch, who is one of the guards. Put him in the treasure room and have him make a list and start boxing everything up. Be sure to tell him that once he is done we will want him to take everything to his bank."

Clark talked to Mark with his mind and told him about the two brothers that were working with the intruders. "Mitch and his brother have taken the mark."

"Don't worry Clark, I'll take care of it."

"Lois, take your people down into the tunnel where the last thermo unit was found, start walking towards the end of the tunnel. Mark will come and take your people down on the sled to your chambers out in the Mediterranean."

"Mark, hide the entrance to the tunnel when you come up from the library with your mind ability and do the same when you go down to take Petra's people to their chamber. Wait there until the intruders have left. Jodie and I will take the planes and fly around until you tell us they've gone."

Jodie and Kent took off in the planes and flew around Casablanca. It really was a beautiful city with old mosques like Hassan II. New modern day hotels, golf courses, a playground for the rich. Kent saw the troop trucks heading for the hangers and told Mark, "You've got about ten minutes before they will be all over the hangers."

The trucks came right through the gates and they went flying in all directions.

"These guys really must want us bad since they don't care how much damage they do."

Twelve truckloads of troops surrounded the two hangers, doors were kicked in, grenades thrown in ahead of the troops. They were really making a mess of things. The officer in charge was yelling orders out to his men.

"Bring all the people you find dead or alive and put them in this truck. We will take them back to headquarters and torture them until we get all the information needed to stop these people from Atlantis. We will find out where they are and how to kill all of them. When we're done with them they will take the mark and then we will cut their heads off."

After a short time the troops came out of the hangers. Walls had been taken down, holes drilled in the floors, scanners listening for anyone talking or moving around, but no one was found.

"Those two brothers must have found some money that belonged to this movie star Jodie and taken it, and are making up stories to cover their butt. They said we would find lots of people here and two old seaplanes and bags full of money. The one brother named Mitch was going to wait at the gate and open it up when we came."

"He wasn't at the gate and we can't find either brother. Let's go back to headquarters and wait till he calls in or we find him. I think the two brothers are just con artists. If they are, their heads are coming off."

"Mark, get the hanger doors open, the intruders are gone and we're on the way down. We need to get in right away as they have planes in the air with heat censers looking for us." They came in for a landing and went right into the hangers and closed the doors.

"We have a lot of work to do on the planes, those bullets hit just about every part of them. Atlantis has a lot of work to do as we're out of missiles and shells. We're also going to need more food for all the people, plus everything else that they couldn't bring along, like toothbrushes, medicines."

One guy said, "Don't forget the beer and make it Coors light."

"Then look at all the work we need to do inside the hangers. Mark came up from the Mediterranean tunnel with the new sled, so we now have a sled for each tunnel. We've got a lot of things coming up on the Teleport, the sleds will be running day and night moving people and supplies. We now have a lot of people to help us get these jobs done. Once the thermo units come, we can install them and start transporting our people to Atlantis where they will be safe from the traitors and the intruders."

After a few days with all the help, they had the work done. The planes were ready to go again, with the new guided missiles and armor piercing bullets.

"Mark, how's our boy Mitch doing with the treasures he's putting into the twelve boxes?"

"He's got them all done and has put his seal on the locks to keep anyone from taking out what he has listed for each box."

"Why don't you go get him and the twelve boxes, Mark. We want him to take this to the bank for safekeeping. When Mitch was sleeping last night we switched the twelve boxes with ones that came apart at the top just like his and put his tops on twelve boxes full of nice colored rocks.

"We've got a pickup outside ready to go, help him put his boxes into the truck. Tell him we would like a signed slip from the bank for our boxes."

"You bet, I'll bring one back as soon as I can, see you guys real soon."

Clark had two men waiting in Casablanca, one at the bank and the other at the intruders' headquarters. Mitch went right to the intruders with his twelve boxes. He went in and they came back out with him all excited.

"The hangers are all full of people and two old seaplanes, you could go there right now and capture them. All I want is one million dollars right now as my reward for this information and you can have the boxes in the pickup that are worth about 100 million. There is a room so full of treasure you could fill ten dump trucks and you can have that, too."

"Let us see what you have in the boxes Mitch. If it's true what you say, we will give you two million and fly you to any place in the world that you want to go to."

"They are all sealed and this the list of what's in each box, there is no need to open them, don't you trust me?"

"Open the box or die, Mitch."

Mitch broke the seal on the lock and said, "Go ahead and open it up, here's the list."

The big guy with the sword looked in the box and took out some rocks. They broke open the seals on the other boxes. Just rocks. Swoosh, off came the head.

"Don't you think we should tell the boss and go check out the hangers again?"

"We didn't find anything last time and this nut said the rocks were gold. You go tell the boss that there's no gold, just rocks and this nut with no head said there was gold and the hangers are full of people. I kind of like my head right where it is. You can go and when the boss asks me where you are I will tell him. I think we will just stay away from the hangers, as this is the second time he told us that the hangers were full of people."

When the two men got back from town, they told Mark and Clark what had happened and that no one was coming to the hangers.

The three guards arrived back to the hangers with their wives and kids. Mark took them down to location 4 on the sled and set them up into their own quarters.

"Please make yourself at home, we have a meeting to go to

and we should be back shortly."

"Mark, let's get everyone together for a meeting, Jodie has come up with a good idea on how to get the power belts to the other 36 leaders."

Everyone that could walk and wasn't hurt got on the sleds and went up to the main hanger.

"Go ahead Jodie, the floor is yours."

"We're going to take the cell phones when they get back from Atlantis and call all 36 people that are on the list from Atlantis who will get the power belts. The cell phones are being worked on so that they can't be traced when you're using them. We are going to send them invitations to play in a golf tournament May 25, 2018 in Casablanca, at the California Golf Resort that will read, "All accommodations, food and drinks, airline tickets will be paid for by the airline. Your airline tickets will come in the mail with your time of departure. We don't want anyone to be late for this three week, all expenses paid vacation. You can bring your kids, dogs or your mother-in-law, that's up to you. The tickets will cover all your kids and four other family members. We will have special gifts for everyone, so be sure to come. Jodie, Mark Doolittle, Clark Kent and Lois Lane will be your hosts. Looking forward to meeting all of you on the 25th of May."

"When they are brought from the airport to the resort, we will have our own Special Forces at the golf course to protect us all from the intruders and the traitors of Atlantis. We will pass out gold coins to all the older people and toys to all the kids. We will then take the 36 people on the list to the conference room and screen them out for the mark of the Antichrist. If they pass the test we will give them the power belts. Once they put the belt on we will tell them how it works and that they are people from Atlantis. They will all start talking to each other with their minds. At first it will be overwhelming to them, but they will soon get use to the belt."

The planes started to arrive from all over the world with luggage, wives, kids, dogs and all 36 Atlanteans and their special guests. The buses were busy bringing them to the resort where the hosts greeted them. Everything went according to the plans that Jodie had laid out. Everyone had been screened out, no one had taken the mark.

They all had their power belts and knew how to use them and were looking forward to getting their people back to Atlantis. Everyone was now enjoying their vacation. Some were just sitting by the pool drinking, others were golfing, scuba diving and gambling.

After two weeks of everyone being on vacation, a message came in from Atlantis.

RED ALERT Date - June 8, 2018 RED ALERT

"Citizens of Atlantis you might find it hard to believe what the Elders of Atlantis have just told our people here in the center of the earth. Jesus Christ the Son of God has just told the Elders to build a large Teleport, so that your people can be teleported to the New Jerusalem that God is building for the people of the Earth whose names are written in the Book of Life.

"The new city is a cube, 1,500 miles in all directions. There are no cubes in outer space; this city is one of many worlds that are in our Milky Way Galaxy that will snap into place on this large globe that will be named THE MILKY WAY GALAXY. All the cities in this globe will have twelve gates each so that they can travel all around in their globe. As time goes by this globe will be attached to other globes and we can travel into these others through the point of attachment. Just think, there are over 500 billion galaxies that we can see, with more being built by God.

"The reason we are being given this great honor is that all our people after the Rapture said that they now believe that Jesus is the Son of God. We never knew Jesus Christ as we were in the center of the earth after the great flood. But we were the lost tribe of the Jewish people that God had put on this earth.

"We are to start building this larger Teleport right away. We also need to build seven new thermo units to be placed in the seven locations to bring our people here to the center of the earth so we can Teleport them to the new city. We must also send up everything our people will need to survive up into the library by using the small Teleport. We will have about 1,260 days from the date of the Rapture, which was May 12, 2018, to get everything ready to start sending our people to our new home. That future date is Sat, Oct. 23, 2021.

"We will continue our vacations before we send out the 36 Atlantis citizens who now have their power belts. All the people that came in with them will be taken a few at a time

IN SEARCH OF Ancient Atlantis

to the hanger until they're all there and taken into the tunnels. The intruders will think that they were just another part of the Rapture. They will also think that all the people left on the earth after the Rapture didn't believe in Jesus Christ. Just as soon as the two Prophets and their 144,000 workers can be killed, they will give them all the mark of the Antichrist or cut their heads off. The clock is now ticking."

Date - June 15, 2018

The 36 were now boarding the planes and heading home to choose the people that they would take back to Atlantis. It wasn't an easy choice, as the rest would have to face the Antichrist and his mark.

"The people that are left are not alone, they have the two Prophets and 144,000 Jewish workers that will put a seal on their foreheads if they believe In Jesus Christ. They won't be hurt by the plagues during the Tribulation, but will have to give up their lives and their heads at the end. The last three and a half years will be hell on earth as His church and the Antichrist will be asking you to convert and take the mark, but it's better to lose your head then your soul."

When the 36 Atlanteans got on the plane, they were told by the Elders, "Go home and find all the people you want to take back with you. Don't tell any of them that you're going to take them home to Atlantis. Let them all think that they are going on a vacation next year or in the near future and that it will be free. Tell them you're looking at seven different locations and that you will give them two days to get ready when it's time to go on vacation. They can bring only one suitcase and what's on the list that you will send to them in the mail. Everything else will be given to you when you arrive at your vacation spot."

Clark also instructed them, "Be sure to screen out all the people that you want to bring home; some will have the mark of the Antichrist. If they find out what you're up to, we will have to come and take you out. You will only have a few hours to get ready, as they are everywhere. You will have to fight your way out to the pick up location. We will be bringing you guns and ammunition as soon as they come up from Atlantis to your exit locations.

"Till then, keep a low profile by going to their meetings and letting them think you're on their side. They won't try to force you to take the mark of the Antichrist until the last three and a half years of the Tribulation. We hope to have everyone back to Atlantis to be teleported to God's new city before those last years.

"The Elders have sent up four new engines and all the equipment needed to put two more seaplanes into operation. These planes will be for Jodie and Lois to fly, as each plane must now pick up the nine Atlanteans who have the power belts and the forty people that they have selected. All four pilots must now sit down and choose which ones they will pick up.

"The first letter of your name will be in front of the nine you have chosen. When they call you or talk to you with their minds they will say this is Johnny or he will say this is M1 and Mark will know it's Johnny, who's number one on his list. Do not call them by their last name; only use their first name or their coded name as they are picking up our signals and they won't know who M1 is. Their last name is coded, Johnny's is 141; only Jodie knows their last names from the codes. Also don't talk over thirty seconds or they will be able to find your location."

Date - July 2, 2018
(Message from Atlantis)

"It's taken more time for our design team to make a thermo unit from the old one, as a lot of the parts were rusted out. We now only have enough material left to build four units.

"The four thermo units should be done some time in 2019. We will keep you updated on the date we will have these done. You will put the four thermo units in the following locations when they are finished.

London. 51.30°N and 0.07°W.

Egypt. 30.47°N and 31.00°E.

The Library. 10°W and 35°N.

The Mediterranean. 36°N and 4°W.

"We also have been working on the larger Teleport and it's taking longer then we anticipated as our people are spread out working on all the things that need to be done."

Estimated time of completion: June 20, 2020

"Guns, ammunition and bulletproof vests and lots of money to buy small companies to hide your people in, are now coming up on the Teleport from the library and are being loaded onto the four planes. We must now move all 36 people who have power belts and the people they want to take with them to four different locations. We need them a lot closer as time will be running out because our factory is way behind on production and it will be real close to the last three and a half years."

"M1 this is Mark, I need you to move your people to Paris and wait there until the thermo unit is completed. Be sure to get the other eight people that have the power belts and their forty people that are on your list. I will talk to you again when I find out more from the Elders. Don't move them all at the same time, we don't want to set up a pattern as they will be checking on anything that is not normal. Buy some small shops, bookstores to put your people to work. Let me know when you're all set up and I'll come in with the needed supplies."

"OK Mark, this is Johnny M1, will do."

"M1, just say Johnny or M1 not both names."

"You're getting too fussy Mark, just too fussy!"

"Jodie, Clark and Lois, I want you to call your people and have them move to their new locations. We will deliver the guns and money as soon as they make the move."

"Sounds good Mark, we will get the job done."

New   Locations

Paris for Mark's nine people, Rome for Jodie, Alexandria for Clark and Athens for Lois.

"Mark this is Johnny M1 at new location, ready to go. Sorry, I forgot, it's just me."

"We will be there on the Seine by the Eiffel Tower in six hours. Get a nice size boat, as we're bringing supplies for all of your nine plus their forty people. Paint the words, Vacation Special on both sides of the boat. See you in six, out, Mark."

"You two guards get on the plane. Jodie, I will need your help with the missiles and the radar system. Clark and Lois you're on stand by. Get your plane ready to go just in case another call comes in."

Mark took off for Paris; the next stop would be the Bay of Biscay to refuel, then on to Paris. The trip was going as planned. Not one intruder on the radar until they got to Paris and then they seemed to be everywhere.

Mark flew over the Seine and talked to M1 with his mind.

"Is it clear to come in for a landing?"

"It's clear Mark," M1 said.

"Just set it down next to the boat that says Vacation Specials."

"It was a good idea of yours to also put the lettering on the plane. They will think we're just part of the tourists coming to see the Eiffel Tower."

Mark set the plane down next to the boat and cut the engines and was soon tied up to the boat. Johnny came right into the plane and told his people to get everything loaded into the boat and fast.

"Glad to meet you Mark, who's this beautiful copilot? She looks just like Jodie Foster."

"Quit messing around Johnny, you know it's not Jodie Foster. I'm in love with Jodie, so keep your distance my friend."

"Take it easy Doolittle, I was just having a little fun."

"The Elders want you and your people to blend into Paris until they get the thermo units finished. If you get into trouble, go to your departure site and call me. But remember, it will take at least six hours to get back here. So get your people trained on the proper use of the weapons, you might have to hold them off till we arrive. Looks like your people got everything on the boat. Will be talking to you in the near future. Be on guard, as some of your people might take the big rewards offered by the intruders and turn you in. Good luck Johnny, hope to see you in a few months."

"Take over Jodie, I'm going to try and get some sleep, wake me if I'm needed."

It had been a good day as no one had even come out to see what they were doing. They were now in the air heading back to Casablanca. When they landed back at the hanger, Mark was still sleeping. Jodie had flown the plane all the way back.

Everyone went into a waiting mode as the thermo units would not be done until some time in 2019.

Date - April 15, 2019

"Mark, this is M1, Mathew M5 is being overrun by intruders

and the traitors of Atlantis. They are fighting it out right now, we can't get to them to help, as there are just too many of them. Mathew told me that one of his people took the mark and turned them in for the reward. The traitor." He also told them that a lot more people from Atlantis have moved into Paris and opened up shops.

"'Don't even try to come and help Johnny or you will be lost, too.' That's the last I heard from Mathew. He said my last name by mistake and they will now be looking for me. I think you should come for all your people, Mark. I'm sorry, I told Mathew my last name. It won't happen again."

"You're right Johnny. We will pick up four of your team leaders and their people at the Seine. All four planes will be there in six hours."

"Let's get the planes filled up and the guards on board. We've each got six hours there and six hours back. It could be longer, if they find out somehow when we're coming and where. Their equipment is getting a lot better and with the help of turncoats they are finding out more things about us and our abilities."

"M1 this is Mark. You better find another location for your next group of people that we need to pick up beside the Seine. Once they see all the planes and boats at the Seine with the Vacation Specials signs all over them they will send people out to check. We won't have much time to get everyone into the planes. Johnny, we should be just about over you in five to ten minutes so get your people ready."

"Mark, we have four boats armed and ready to protect you from the intruders when you land."

Date - April 15, 2019 Time - 9:30 PM

"This is it, follow me down to the boats and be ready to fire on anything that comes our way."

All four planes landed and came up alongside the boats. As they tied up to them, floodlights came on from shore and other boats started to race out towards them. All hell broke loose as guns from both sides lit up the night. It was a good thing everyone was well-armed, even at that they took some hits to the planes and some of the people were wounded. All the boats from shore were burning in the water. All their people were now in the planes.

"Let's get out of here, we've got a lot of boats coming at us from up and down the river."

"That's not all Mark, look at your radar screen. I can't count all the planes and helicopters coming at us."

"Turn towards the Eiffel Tower team, we will need full power to get them airborne before we hit the shore."

Mark pulled back on the steering wheel and the old tub just cleared the beach.

"Keep them low over Paris so their guns can't fire at us. Jodie you follow me, Clark and Lois, we will see you back at the hangers, good luck to everyone."

"Mark, Johnny here at the Seine. I got into a two-man sub and went upriver to get away from the intruders. We will help the others get ready for when you can come back for all of us. You have all M2 through M4 people on your planes. The bad news is that M5 and all his people went down fighting, but they took a lot of them with them. The good news is, no one took the mark of the Antichrist. They were told to surrender or die, and they choose to die for Christ."

Seven hours later the planes came in from the Seine and started to land at the hangers.

Clark and Lois were the first ones to get their people unloaded. They had nine people that were wounded, one had died on the way back. They were beginning to worry about the other planes as another four hours had gone by since they landed.

Then they could hear one plane coming in with the engines missing and making a loud popping noise. Mark came in for a hard landing and blew out two tires and slid to a stop. All the people were taken off the plane, some were carried into the sick bay where doctors and nurses were waiting. A work crew then came out and pulled the plane into the hanger to be worked on.

Date - April 16, 2019 Time - 10 AM

"What happened Mark? Where's Jodie?"

"The intruders have a new weapon. They can send out electrical beams towards our planes that can shut down our conversations and burn up some of the wires if they can lock in on us. I was lucky that I could turn away from the beam. Jodie was telling me that her plane was starting to miss real badly and that's when we couldn't talk to each other. I tried to stay by her plane until she could land it in the water next to Palma. When she landed a lot of boats came out and were towing her plane into Palma. I could hardly keep flying and had no choice but to come back to the hangers.

"Have our electrical engineers find out which wires were burned up on my plane. It must be a certain material in the engine wires as all the other wires seem to be OK. I will need those wires made up right away. Get the other planes ready to go with the new wires put in all of them. They will be able to stop our conversations but not the planes. Have one set of wires for Jodie's plane made up just in case we have time to repair the plane. Get the two best mechanics you have and put them on my plane, just in case I need them.

"Get the best gunners and long range sharp shooters for the heavy 50-caliber sniper rifles and mount ten extra rockets on your plane, Clark. I'll bring forty well-armed Commandos for my plane, I'm going to need them. We will have to fight our way into Jodie's plane. We are now down to three planes that are flyable, so pray to Jesus for help, we're going to need it."

"Mark we can only talk for thirty seconds, they have us locked up in a large building in Palma, I will talk to you later today. Don't try to talk to me," Jodie said.

"Jodie just talked to me, they have them locked up in Palma. We will take off as soon as the wires are finished. We've got to get them out along with the plane or we're going to lose a lot of people."

"Mark, don't try to come for us, they are going to cut our heads off in the morning if we don't take the mark. They've got too many intruders around the Palma Royal Nautical Club. They also have a lot of boats, planes and helicopters loaded with troops on standby."

The Elders of Atlantis told Mark that they could only make two thermo units as time and materials were both running out.

New locations for two instant thermo units

Put the first one at 36°N and 4°W out in the Mediterranean.
Put the second one at 25.59°N and 10.33°E by Sardalas, Libya.

"Mark, have your people bring up the instant thermo units on the power sleds and take one down in the tunnel that goes down to the location in the Mediterranean. Get it hooked up and operational, as it will be needed to transfer all the people to Atlantis. We won't have enough room for everyone at the hangers and the intruders might come back.

"Take the other one by truck to the new location in Libya. The Elders have used their lasers to make a tunnel right up to the ancient buildings. Have Tom M3 and George M4 get twelve good men to go along with you just in case they are needed. Travel only at night. When you get there, hook it up per the instructions listed on the machine.

"The wires will be ready for all the planes by 11 PM today. We will take off as soon as the three planes are wired. It's going to be close, we won't be there over Palma until about 4 AM tomorrow on the 17 of April. It won't take us long to get there once we're in the air. Remember, we don't take any prisoners. Be sure to take them out before they can tell anyone that we're there to get our people out. It will take about an hour to rewire Jodie's plane so we've got to get all the people back from the club to the planes by then."

"It's time, the wires are fixed, let's get into the air and get this job done. Clark, you and Lois will be flying cover for us, you will have to keep all their people off us. When we get there, I'll land right at the boat club and fight our way into the building."

It didn't take long to fly there from the hangers.

"We're here, Clark. I'm going down into the bay, wish me luck."

Mark could see Jodie's plane at the dock as he came in for a landing. There were only a few guards at the boat and they didn't seem to be concerned as he pulled up next to the plane. Twenty Commandos were all over them before they even had a chance to defend themselves.

"You men stay here and protect the mechanics when they install the wires on Jodie's plane. You other men come with me, we're going to get our people out of that club. I talked to Jodie and told her that were coming in."

"How do we know which ones are our people?" one of the men asked.

"Jodie said all her people will raise their right hand above their heads. No right hand above their heads, shoot them. Move fast as they have our people in many different rooms."

As they fought from room to room, people on both sides were being wounded and killed. Fighting went on for about thirty minutes then all went silent.

The only noise was the wounded calling for help and the

shots coming from the dock. Jodie came running up to Mark and gave him a big hug.

"I'm glad you came, but they have been waiting for you. There's just too many of them. I heard one of the officers say, 'We will kill all of them, they will never get out of here alive.'"

"Let's just see about that! Help all the wounded back to the dock, leave the dead as they are now in God's hands. You men that are not wounded clear a path back to the planes. Get all the wounded into my plane. Jodie will take off with Tom and give us additional cover. I'll stay here until the wires are done."

Clark was calling for help when the intruders turned on their electrical beams. No one could talk to each other with their minds and radios were worthless. Planes and helicopters were falling out of the skies in flames and rockets were coming in from the old tubs taking out troops that were coming down to the docks in trucks. One of the mechanics was hit and fell into the water. He was pulled from the water and put into the plane. He told the commando that he was done, but the engine cover had to be put back on. The other mechanic said he was done as he came off the right wing.

"I'll go put the cover on, you tell Mark to get everyone on the plane and let's get the 'H' out of here."

Everyone got into the plane except the mechanic, since he was hit as he was running back to get in. He slid off the wing into the water and never came back up.

Mark started the engines and put full power on both engines as the plane seemed to take forever to clear the water. A boat was coming at them with guns locked in and ready to fire as Mark sent a rocket into the bridge. They flew right through a ball of fire that set the wheels on fire. Mark had to go back down to the water to put the fires out. That's when a jet came in for the kill. Mark couldn't call for help as the electrical beam was still on. He thought it was all over, but a rocket sped right by his plane into the jet. Jodie flew next to his plane with a big smile on her face. She pointed in the direction of the hangers and rocked her wings back and forth.

After a short time Jodie came in for a landing. She was already inside the hanger, unloading her people when Mark landed.

"Let's get all the people that aren't wounded down to the thermo unit and transfer them to Atlantis. As soon as we can get the wounded stable enough to move them down through the tunnel to be transferred, do it. We all have to be gone by high noon.

"Tom, keep all the Commandos that aren't wounded in the hanger as you will be taking them and the thermo unit that's down in the tunnel by truck to location 30.47°N and 31.00°E in Egypt, just as soon as everyone else is transferred."

Mark could hear the last plane coming in and thought, "God gave us help, as there was no way we should have all gotten back."

"Let's get the planes and everyone into the hangers and all the people fixed up first. Send all the people to Atlantis that aren't needed. I will need a report on how many people were lost and wounded. Get everyone back working on the planes as we will have to go to Paris to find M1 and all his people. All planes must be well-armed as this will be another firefight to the end."

"We got hit real bad Mark, 18 people were killed, six of them were Commandos and twenty other people were wounded and twelve of them couldn't be moved until the doctors could work on them. We also lost our two best electrical engineers, one was killed and the other we had to send down to Atlantis as he was wounded real bad."

"The Elders are sending up two more engineers and two large desert tents to hide the planes in at the two locations out in the deserts. They also said we must be gone by noon, as the intruders and the traitors are checking on where to find this Jodie person.   It won't be long before they find out that she was making a movie at Casablanca."

They now had everyone sent to Atlantis and the thermo unit was being loaded onto M3's truck along with the engineers and tents. They also had four other trucks loaded with everything that they would need to survive for the next four years. Mark told them to leave and go to a deserted warehouse close by and wait until dark.

"Only travel at night in the old army trucks, as they will draw too much attention. Take the last 34 Commandos with you. Good luck Tom, hope to see you in a few days."

"Let's seal up both tunnels with the laser beams and get this place cleaned up. We don't want them to know we were here. Pull the planes out of the hanger and lock the doors. We won't be coming back here again as this is where they will be looking for Jodie."

The planes were in the air heading for Paris to pick up M1 when the intruders arrived and were all over the hangers. They started to bulldoze the buildings down and dig holes in all the floors looking for underground tunnels. Mark turned his scanner on his radio to see if he could pick up their conversation. He could hear the Captain tell the air base that they didn't find anything.

"No one's been in this place for years, I'm coming back to base."

"M1 this is Mark, get your people down to the Seine by the Eiffel Tower by 6 PM today. Spread them out four miles apart up and down the river. We will then be able to give you fire cover. There shouldn't be too many intruders or traitors there as they would never guess we would come back there again."

"Kent and Lois talk to your people while we're flying to Paris and have them slowly move everyone to Rome on their vacations. Have them settle down in the countryside out of sight of the big cities and the intruders. We must move everyone to Cairo and Alexandria before the last three and a half years of the Tribulation. The intruders will demand travel permits to go anywhere, even from town to town, let alone to another country. We all must go into hiding and slowly move all our people to C and A. Jodie, also talk to your people and have them slowly start moving their people right away to Cairo and Alexandria. We're all going into hiding, out in the desert where Patton and Rommel first met face to face."

"Johnny, we are coming up and down the river towards the Eiffel Tower, are you in position?"

"Yes, but we're being chased by lots of boats, Mark."

"We will take them out and circle back and land, so get your people ready to jump into the planes. We want to be back in the air in two minutes as our radar is starting to pick up planes."

They went in with the rockets locked in on the boats, which were soon all on fire heading for the bottom. The planes pulled up to the boats and in less then two minutes everyone was loaded. The planes had to fly under the bridges to gain speed for takeoff. It was close but they all made it. All the planes turned for the incoming jets and fired their missiles, then turned again and flew low over Paris towards the Mediterranean. The missiles ran true; not one plane was after them.

"That's the best we've ever done against the intruders, not one person was even hurt. We will all set down to refuel out in the Mediterranean. Only one plane at a time will land to refill as they might find us. When we can't talk to each other we will know that they have found us."

"Something's wrong Mark, I can feel it in my bones," Jodie said. "We haven't seen one plane on our radar even when we flew by the airports."

"I think they have found a way to track us and to make their planes invisible to us. Let's land in the bay and tie all our planes together. Have everyone that has a power belt stand on the wings and use their ability number four and five together to put a force field around us and the planes. Let's refuel the planes at the same time."

"I think someone on one of the planes has turned traitor and has a tracking device on them. Have our trusted guards from the hangers find out who it is and throw the tracking device and the person or persons overboard."

It wasn't too long and they could hear two people being thrown into the water.

"Did you kill them?"

"No, the sharks will."

Jodie was right, the planes were now overhead looking for them, but the radar was blank. The planes were soon going in all directions trying to find them as their abilities had made the planes invisible.

"Get the radar people working on our radar. I think if we change impulses we can make it work again. They can't cover all the ranges and impulses."

"Mark you're right, it's working again and we can see their planes."

"Let me know when they're gone, they will have to go back for fuel."

It was at least an hour before all the planes left.

"It's all clear Mark," Kent said as he was looking at the radar screen.

"OK let's take off, but keep just a hundred feet off the water."

"Kent and Petra land at 30.47°N and 31.00°E in Egypt and unload your people. Keep only the best men and women to protect the planes and the tunnel and send the rest down to Atlantis. Jodie and I will go to 25.59°N and 10.33°E and do the same thing. We now must go into hiding and let things settle down. Our people will slowly come to Cairo and Alexandria on vacation from Rome. We will again screen them out as we pick them up to insure that no one has any cell phones or anything that can tell the intruders where we are taking them."

Date - April 18, 2019

"I'm sure as time goes by they will find out where we are. But they will pay for every foot out in the sand with their lives. We will set up so many guns and tank traps that it will take them a day to just go a few miles. Then when they get close, we will laser the tunnel shut and take the thermo unit back to the hanger and open up both tunnels, hook it up again as it was before. The Elders will be sending up a lot more weapons and people if needed from the library. Put Tom in charge of the troops and of taking the thermo unit back to the hangers if needed."

Date - March 15, the ides of March, 2020

"Time has gone by slowly since we moved to Libya and Egypt. Our people are still coming in from Rome and are starting to come in from other countries. Someone has let the cat out of the bag and soon the mice will be coming after the cat, and that's us. There are two important dates that we are waiting for and one better get here soon. The first date is very, and I mean very, important."

THE FIRST DATE - june 20, 2020

"This is when the Teleport should be ready and we can start sending our people to the new city of Jerusalem that God has made for all the people of the Earth that believe in him and his Son and the Holy Spirit. A lot of people who didn't know God, but were good people and did good work here on Earth, will also be judged at the last Judgment by God and will also make it to the new city. This city is a 1500-mile cube. There are no cubes in outer space, only round planets. So this cube will be inserted into a round planet that will be called the Milky Way Galaxy. We will learn more about this later in time."

THE SECOND DATE - OCT. 23, 2021

The last three and a half years.

"Kent, have Denzel M6 and Angelina M7 take twenty Commandos each and set them up with the anti-tank guns and rockets in Egypt. Jodie have Liam M8 and Sean M9 do the same thing at their location in Libya. We must protect our thermo units at these locations."

Date - june 20, 2020

"The Teleport is finished right on time and is now sending people to the new city. Send only the people that can't be used here on Earth to help us and Israel fight the intruders and the traitors of Atlantis."

"The first thing we must do, is trace out the location of the electrical beam that is sending out signals that are burning up our wires and stopping us from using our radar and communication with each other. It must be destroyed at all cost."

"The Elders have found the location of the electrical beam. It's at the airport in Palma and is being sent from there around the world to satellites."

"We will need four well-trained Commando teams and a good leader for each team. Each leader will hand pick forty people for his or her team from the people that have made it from Rome. These people are now at the two locations out in the deserts. These Commandos will set their watches so that they will hit the target at the same time as they come in from all directions in the four old planes. The Elders say that only 50% of them will make it back alive. If you are chosen as a leader you can turn it down, no one will know but you and the Elders. Any Commando that says no will be sent to Israel and put in the lead tank when he gets there. This was the way Patton took care of these matters and it seemed to work."

"Only leaders that are pilots will be chosen since our main pilots of these planes have earned a rest. The following list will be given out to the four people who stepped forward to take on this important job. The people of Atlantis and Israel take pride in saying that you are the very best citizens any nation could have. Good luck to all."

"Meg, who was one of the pilots, got sick. Jodie said she would take her place."

"Jodie and Nicolas K4, you will leave from the desert location in Egypt. Get your planes and people ready to go. Each plane will have two extra guards to fire the guns when you come in for a landing."

"William P2 and Kevin P5, you will leave from the desert location in Libya, get your plane and people ready. You're going to be there by dark on July 4. We're going to give them the fear of being hunted."

Date - July 4, 2020

The four planes were now airborne and would fly into Palma at night, hitting the airport at the same time. They all lined up at their locations; it was timed to the last second. In they came, heading for the control tower where the electrical beam was in operation. Guns and rockets were fired at planes, troops and communication centers. One old plane went down in flames but landed in a field by the tower. The Commandos came running out of the plane and were fighting their way to the tower when the plane blew up. No one else was seen getting out as the other three planes landed next to the tower. Two Commando teams went into the tower as the others took up fire positions

The Commandos set their charges in the tower and ran back to their aircraft just as the planes from Israel came over the airport and took out all the planes on the ground and any that got into the air. The tower went up in flames when charges went off.

"Mark, this is K4 can you hear me?"

"You did it, we can hear you and again we will be able to talk to everyone that has a power belt."

"This is Kevin, Mark. William's plane went down and the only ones that got out were the Commandos."

"Get back to your planes, pick up all survivors and get the hell out of there. The planes from Israel are heading back and must hook up with the air tankers. You are now alone, good luck my friends, over and out, Mark."

"Kurt J4 and his team are calling for help as they are being chased down a highway near Barletta, Italy. Kevin, see if you can pick up Kurt's team and bring them back with you. Just forget their call codes and call everyone by their name, it looks like they have found out who we all are, they must have gotten the list from a traitor."

Information From Israel

"Israel has given us four submarines to help pick up our people since they have fled Rome and are now hiding on many islands in the Mediterranean. The intruders seem to be everywhere, checking all boats, even cruise ships. People are being taken into their prisons from the boats and tortured until they give up someone, anyone to the intruders and tell them that they know for sure that these people are from Atlantis. A lot of innocent people are being killed, but a few of our people have been traced down and had to fight it out with the intruders.

"We will need two leaders on each sub with their Commandos to hit certain ports and get our people back home. The following people will be trained in all positions in the subs: Sub 101 Brad and Matt; Sub 102 Steve and Diane; Sub 103 Harrison and Morgan; Sub 104 Kevin and Will.

"The intruders have issued a list of all the people they have killed. They have put this list on the Internet worldwide. They're telling everyone, 'If you know who the Atlantis people are and haven't turned them in or are hiding them, when we find out we will cut your heads off, along with theirs.'

"We regret to tell you that the following three leaders and their people have been killed: Emma and her people near Rome went down fighting; it was said that over 500 intruders went down with them. Harry and all of his people, the report said they never got to fire one shot as a jet took out the small boat they were on. Jeff and his people were turned in as they were on a train from Rome to Naples. They were going to take a cruise ship to Egypt and didn't have any guns with them. All were taken alive, no one took the mark, they all lost their heads."

Date - July 6

"Kurt, this is Kevin, we should be over Barletta in thirty minutes. Try to get to Porto Commerciale Di Barletta and hold them off. We will come in with three planes; two will stay in the air to give us plenty of cover. Flash your lights on and off and I will come right to shore where you are. My Commandos will help any wounded people into the plane. We have to be fast, as our radar shows lots of planes around Barletta."

"Make it fast Kevin, as we are about twenty minutes from

that location and we are running out of ammunition. There will be two trucks full of troops not too far behind us, I just hope you make it in time. If you don't, do me a favor. Blow the hell out of them."

It seemed like an hour but it was just thirty minutes. Kevin came in low at the port hoping to see flashing lights. The guard who was manning one of the guns yelled, "Over there, I see the lights flashing." Kevin turned towards the lights and could see two trucks coming down the road towards Kurt. He told the other planes to take them out and any planes that might be coming their way. The plane came in right up to the shore, Kevin's men were out of the plane helping the wounded into the plane, and the medical teams started working on them. They were soon back into the air and could see the trucks burning on the road.

"Let's head back to our locations in the desert. It's been a good two days people, we didn't lose as many as they thought we would."

They were soon coming in for a landing at both locations and told their ground crews to bring the ambulances as they had a lot of people in need of emergency treatment. Soon everyone was now inside the chambers and the planes were under cover and being worked on.

Everyone must now wait until people were trained in the proper use of submarines and glider planes.

Date - Nov. 25, 2020

Since the Rapture on May 12, 2018, the Antichrist, the leader of the intruders and the traitors of Atlantis, had given Israel permission to rebuild their temple. He also signed a seven-year treaty with them guaranteeing their safety. The temple will be finished just as the last three and a half years of the Tribulation start. That date is on the minds of all the people of the Earth, Oct. 23, 2021.

Mark Doolittle is having trouble remembering dates and people's names. The doctors thought it was from a concussion that he got when his plane hit the runway and tore the wheels off. They are taking him down to Atlantis where he will receive a hero's welcome for a job well done. Jodie was told by the Elders, "You will see him again."

The new leaders will now be Kent Patton and Petra Rommel, who would talk to all the power belt holders and set up all attacks on the intruders. More people will have to be trained in the many different operations that will be going on.

The list of things to be done would grow, but these people would get the job done. They will stay at the desert locations as other pilots will now fly the planes to give them a rest.

The job List

1. Sandra, you have made it to Alexandria with your people, good job! Your people will all be sent to Atlantis. We now need you to go to the headquarters of the Antichrist in Rome. A fake mark of the beast with your number will be put on your hand. We have broken into their computers and gotten the numbers that they were going to give to our people. We will need all the

information that you can send us with your mind. If they find you out, we won't be able to help you. We all love you, good luck.

2. Megan and Meg you both got all your people to Cairo, a great job well done. You will also go to Rome and report back to Atlantis. Your fake marks will also be put on your hands. You both could end up getting your heads cut off. You both will be in our prayers.

3. We still have a lot of our people to pick up from the different islands they made it to from Rome and where they are now hiding. The intruders have stopped all travel by air or boats. The bulletin issued by them states that a travel permit is now needed to go anywhere in the world. Anyone caught trying to travel without permission will lose their heads.

The following is a list of our people and the Islands they are hiding on.

1. John and Bruce at Pantelleria, La Tortuga Boat rental.
2. Van and Jason at Malta.
3. Brady and Wesley at Lampedusa city, Linosa Bay.
4. Al and Duane at Gavdos, Potamos Beach.

"The last three planes will be set up to pull gliders full of Commandos. The following pilots will now fly the planes: Jodie, Nicolas and Johnny.

"Kevin was injured and had to have metal removed from his back. He still wanted to go, but we sent him down to Atlantis for further treatment.

"We had lost contact with most of our people when the

electrical beam was used by the intruders. Kent was looking for Samuel, since he was the last person heard from when instructed to go to Rome with his people. He got no response because Samuel's power belt had been hit by a bullet when he was attacked by some traitors of Atlantis. He tried to fix it, but the inner parts were burned up. They had to get out of Rome as they were being hunted. He had found an old boat and was taking his people to Egypt when the old thing quit running just off the coast. They could see the intruders' boats coming at them, when a destroyer from Israel maneuvered between them and the other boats and picked them up. They were lucky, as they were then taken to Israel and safety."

People were being trained for all recovery operations. The subs, planes and paratroopers were ready to go. Everyone could again talk to the others that had power belts. Over a period of few months, Kent and Petra had gotten all the people set up and ready to start operation Holy Spirit.

Date - July 20, 2021 - Holy Spirit Day

"Let's get all the subs on their way, as it will take a few days for them to get there.

SUB 101. Go to Pantelleria and pick up John and Bruce at La Tortuga Boat Rental. They will rent boats and come out into the bay when you get there.

SUB 102. Go to Malta and talk to Van and Jason, they will

tell you where to come for them. The intruders are looking for them and will have them surrounded by the time you get there. You will need support from the plane and the Commandos in the gliders. So coordinate your time with Jodie.

SUB 103. Go to Lampedusa City, at Linosa Bay and talk to Brady and Wesley. You will need the support of Nicolas and his Commandos. Call them in when you're ready to pick up the teams.

SUB 104. Al and Dwayne are on Linosa at Via Scalo Vecchio. They are in a shoot out with the intruders and the traitors of Atlantis and will move to the beach when you talk to them. You're going to need Johnny and his plane full of Commandos, plus a glider full of special Commandos that he claims are all descendants of old Blackbeard."

Petra and Kent told all the submarine leaders to let them know when their subs were in position. They needed to coordinate their time with the planes that would be in the air over their positions when they reached them. All subs were instructed to travel underwater and in silent mode. Everyone should be ready in a few days.

Date - July 24, 2021

"The subs are just about in position and are now ready for the planes and support troops to take off. When the planes get to their destinations over top of your positions, they will talk to your leaders."

"This is Brad on Sub 101. John and Bruce are you ready to go?"

"Don't surface Brad, there are two destroyers just off the bay waiting for you and four trucks full of troops waiting for us to get into the boats to come out to you. We would be sitting ducks and we would all be killed. I think we have someone among us that is with the intruders, as they were waiting for you to get here. Find out who it is, we don't want them to come back to Egypt with us."

"I will call for help John and let you know when to come out to the sub."

"Jodie this is Brad, I need you to ask Van where he wants you to drop the glider off at Malta. We need your help at Pantelleria, at La Tortuga boat rental. We only have two destroyers and a few troops for you to take out. Let me know when you get here and I will surface to get the action started."

"Will do Brad, Jodie over and out."

"Van and Jason, this is Jodie, where do you want the glider dropped off? I have to go to Pantelleria to help out Bruce and his people first."

"Drop them off at Margo's at Mistra Bay."

"Will do, I should be back in a few hours, so hold on the best you can."

"Brad, this is Jodie, I'm over the boat rental now."

"Land next to shore and get your Commandos out to protect John and Bruce's people as they come out to the sub. Get your plane back into the air as I'm going to surface. The destroyers will pick me up on their radar and come after me. You must take them out or all will be lost."

"Brad this is Jodie, they're coming in fast and have two helicopters airborne from their ships. I have fired two missiles at the ships and they are on fire and have stopped in the water. The Commandos need help back at the beach as they are being driven back by the troops. You will have to take care of the two helicopters. My radar shows a lot of ships coming at us and I'm estimating they will be here in about twenty minutes."

When Jodie got back to the beach she had to fire her guns into the troops and some of her own men as they were fighting hand-to-hand. Once she got them separated, she took out the rest of the troops and went back to help take out the helicopters.

One of the helicopters had been shot down, but the other one had taken out some of the small boats. It was soon hit by her two gunners and went down in flames.

Jodie turned around and landed back at the beach to pick up her men. Only ten show up carrying six of the wounded; the rest were killed in action. Thirty-six good men had given their lives to protect the others. Two men who didn't get into the boats to go out to the sub, boarded her plane instead.

"I'll check on those two when I get time, right now I have to get out of here," Jodie thought. She took off from the beach and could see on her radar that ships were almost to the bay.

"Brad get your people on the sub, you might have five minutes left. I can't stay as I don't have enough missiles left to stop them, see you back in Egypt."

Off she went, flying just above the water.

"Van, this is Jodie, I'm on the way back now, how are your men holding out?"

"We have been hit real hard, only have twenty good fighting men left of the Commandos that came in on the glider. We will need your forty men to fight them off at the beach when the sub comes in."

"Call the sub in as they have forty Commandos on it. We only have ten men left that can fight, the rest were either killed or are wounded."

"This is Van. Steve or Diane can you hear me?"

"Yes we can, where are you?"

"We need you to come to Margo's, at Mistra Bay and drop your Commandos off so we can get our people who are at the bus station in Xemxija."

"We heard you talking to Jodie when she had to go to Pantelleria. We will surface and put the men on the beach by Margo's, but will have to go back in the bay to dive out of sight."

Jodie was just overhead at Mistra Bay when the sub came in to let the Commandos off.

She turned toward the beach and landed next to the sub. Her ten men got off and got into trucks to go to the bus station. Diane told Jodie that they had to go out in the bay and dive back down as they would be an easy target siting on top of the water.

"Give us a call when you're ready for us to get everyone on the sub."

"Will do Diane, see you soon."

Jodie took off and followed the trucks down the road to Xemxija. The intruders had the bus station surrounded and Jodie took out the ones in front of the bus station. The Commandos fought their way in and moved the people out to the trucks. Jodie killed the other intruders as the trucks left for Margo's. The intruders started following after the trucks but Jodie decimated them. When the trucks got to Margo's, no one was on the road coming after them.

Jodie was just coming in for a landing behind the trucks when she saw a destroyer over the sub dropping depth charges. They didn't have a chance.

"The sub is sunk, it won't be coming to pick your people up. Van and Jason, get all your people and the Commandos into the plane and let's get out of here. When we're in the air I want you to find the two people that got on my plane on the beach at Pantelleria and throw them out the door. One of them has a cell phone and is telling them what we are doing. We can't take the chance, they both must go."

Jodie took off and turned into the direction of the destroyer's and let two missiles go. It was nice to see both of them hit home. It wasn't long before they were burning and heading for the bottom.

"Kent, this is Jodie, we're on the way home from Malta. The 101 is on the way home from Pantelleria. I'm sorry to say we lost the crew of the 102, but we got the Commandos that were put off on shore here on the plane.

"I'm going to meet the 101 out to sea and take the wounded off the sub. All the Commandos will get on the sub in case they are needed to help the others off the other two islands. I should be back in a few hours with all the wounded, the 101 will take a few days."

"This is Sub 103. I'm at Lampedusa city. Wesley and Brady are you ready to go and where are you hiding?"

"It's about time you got here. Two old men running a submarine called the slow boat from China, what will they think of next? They must have run out of young people back there, ones that can get the job done before they die of old age."

"Get too smart and we will let you swim back, isn't that right Morgan?"

"You bet Harrison, all the way back."

"Sorry, we were just having a little fun. We are hiding in a large boat by the northeastern cliffs of Lampedusa and the intruders know we're here. They're waiting for someone dumb enough to try and get us out."

"That's why they sent us Wesley, two old men whose time has just about run out and this was one of the things on our bucket list. So hold on, we're bringing in more help. We will let you know when we're coming in."

"Sub 101, we need your help. Let me know when you're ready Brad."

"I'll be coming into the cliffs in less then ten minutes. We heard your conversation with Wesley. We were heading back to Egypt when we got your call."

"Get ready Wesley, Sub 101 will be there in 10 minutes."

"Bring your sub to the northeastern cliffs of Lampedusa, Brad. We will tell you where to come in and where to put your Commandos onshore. You will then fill your sub with the wounded and the ones not trained for military duty. Once your boat is full, take off for Egypt. We are bringing in more help so that you can get away from the cliffs."

"Nicolas, are you near Lampedusa?"

"We are right over the cliffs as we speak Harrison."

"Unhook your glider and have them land on top of the cliffs. We want you to land in the water and put your Commandos onshore with their rocket launchers. Get back in the air as they will have planes and ships coming at you from all directions."

"Once Sub 101 has left the shore, Wesley, we want you to take all the people off the big boat and send your boat out from the cliffs where you were hiding, with just one man at the controls. Have him jump off the boat and we will pick him up as we come in with Sub 103 to pick up your people you took off the boat."

"We have a message coming in from Linosa at Via Scalo Vecchio, where Al and Dwayne have their people. The intruders have broken off the fight with them and all their planes and destroyers are now heading for Lampedusa. They will be there and on top of you in a very short time."

"Sub 104 is now coming in to pick us up. Kevin and Will have been told to take us to Israel to help fight the Antichrist because he's trying to take over the rebuilt temple."

"John is heading for Lampedusa to help out Wesley and Brady. This will be one hell of a fight as both sides are loaded for bear."

"Nicolas this is Johnny, you have a lot of planes and ships coming your way. I'll hit them from the rear, you get them from the front. We will get them coming and going."

"I'll go to the top of the cliff and cut my glider loose. The Commandos have a lot of firepower to stop any tanks or troops. I will go down to the water and land and put my forty men on the beach with their missiles to take care of planes and ships."

The battle went on for three hours, with people killed in large numbers on both sides. The intruders had 100 times more people killed than the heroes of the day, but the kill rate was just about the same, 100 to one. One of our planes was shot down but only two people got out. Then all at once it was over, dead silence. The only thing you could hear were a few cries for help and the surf hitting the cliffs.

"This is Harrison and Morgan on Sub 103. Whoever is flying the last plane, land at the top of the cliff and hook up your glider. Get all the wounded into your plane and the glider. It's a long flat top on the cliff, you should be able to get airborne. Head back to Egypt and let them know for sure who was lost and who's coming home."

"Harrison, this is Nicolas. I'm on the top of the cliff, Johnny's plane was shot down. When we went back to see if anyone had survived the crash, we found the two guards holding onto the tail section. I'm afraid he went down with the rest of the plane. I'm taking off now and will be heading back too Egypt."

"This is Morgan, let's check everyone on the beach. If they're alive put them in the sub. We must think of the living first. I would like to take them all back, but we've got our orders and the ones still alive must take up what space we have left."

"The Elders have told us to go to Israel along with Sub 104. So hope to see you all in the near future."

The 103 left the cliffs heading for Israel and the future.

Date - July 24, 2021 - Time 6 PM

"Kent and Petra, this is Jodie, I should be coming into Egypt by 10 PM today. I have a lot of people wounded and will need to be unloaded real fast as some of them won't make it much longer. Sub 101 will be coming in July 28 at Alexandria. We will have to pick them up and bring them out to the desert location. They also have a lot of wounded people. I have just heard from Nicolas that Johnny was killed in action, but I've got good news for everyone. Harrison and Morgan have just found this man swimming with the sharks as they left the cliffs. He was about to be eaten when we pulled him from the water. It's him, it's Johnny. He's now on the 101 being treated by our doctors. He's cut up, black and blue and has broken three ribs and his left arm."

"Kent, this is Nicolas, I hope to be coming in just a few hours after Jodie gets there. I have a glider and a plane full of wounded people. We have been putting all our drinking water and our urine into the fuel tanks for fuel. We can't land in the water to refill because we would lose the glider. I'm flying over land, just in case I run out of fuel. If I do, I'll drop the glider and refuel the plane and come in with the wounded. Will keep you updated on our location. You might have to send out a team to the glider."

"We just got some bad news from Sandra, who is in Rome at the headquarters of the Antichrist. Megan has been taken by the intruders to a prison; she was caught looking through some files. They have a way of getting information out of each person they take there. Everyone has a breaking point. Sandra has found out that the intruders are going to move a very large amount of supplies and troops to Alexandria and Cairo. They plan on attacking Israel and taking over the rebuilt temple when it is completed. Petra, I'm getting on the next plane to Cairo with Meg as it won't be safe here. I just hope Megan doesn't break until I get back to Cairo or we will have three heads laying on the ground. Hers, mine and Meg's."

Date - July 24, 2021 - Time 10:15 PM

"Kent, this is Jodie. I'm coming in for a landing in about ten minutes, it's been a long day. I'm trying to stay awake, so you better talk to me until I get down."

"Jodie, you and everyone on your plane will be going down to Atlantis, your work here on Earth will be over when you land. We can see that you're now about to touch down. Our people will take all your people off the plane."

The plane came to a stop just short of the runway. Everyone was taken off the plane when Kent asked, "Where's Jodie?" He went aboard and found her asleep. She was carried off the plane and didn't even wake up.

Petra was on the satellite computer and could see all the ships off the coast of Egypt. They were unloading troops, tanks and everything needed to attack Israel. It would take them at least a month to get all the ships unloaded.

"We better tell Sub 101 to go to Al Ugaylah, Libya. They can't go to Egypt as the intruders are all over that location."

"Sub 101, this is Petra. Go to Al Ugaylah. We will send Liam and Sean at night to pick you up. Let us know when you think you will be there."

"Will do Petra, as soon as Harrison can work out the time and the proper place to come in. We can't surface until we're next to shore or their radar will pick us up. They have this new radar Petra, that can even pick up your planes. So don't send the planes, they will never get here, they will be shot down. This radar was put in operation today at 10 PM. If you had any planes in the air at that time, they will know where you landed. They will be sending troops and tanks out to arrest you. If you fight back they will kill you."

"Thanks for the information Morgan, let us know when you're about there."

"Nicolas, we need you to fly to Al Ugaylah, Libya and drop the glider off right at the water's edge. Fill your plane with fuel and fly to this location in Egypt. The intruders will let you come right in for a landing. They will then attack and try to take us alive.

"Denzel and Angelina will hold them off until we can get everyone down to Atlantis. They have tank traps and mines and twenty Commandos to help them out. Once we're down, they will run for the entrance and use the thermo unit. The last person going down will turn on the laser and seal the entrance. Do not destroy the thermo unit as we will reopen this entrance in the future to send out Special Forces."

As they were running to the entrance, Denzel was hit by a heavy 50-caliber that just about tore him in half. The two planes went up in flames as Angelina ran for the entrance. She had no choice but to send everyone down and turn on the laser.

Date - July 25, 2021 - Time 12:45 AM

"Liam and Sean get your trucks on the road. Leave your Commandos there to protect the entrance. Travel at night only. Go to Al Ugaylah, in Libya and pick up the people from Sub 101 and the people from the glider. Don't take too long as the intruders will be looking for anyone traveling without a permit. Once you get back, send everyone down to Atlantis. The last man will use the laser to destroy the thermo unit and seal the entrance forever. We're at Al Ugaylah, it's getting light, we will wait until it gets dark. Sean can you hear me?"

"This is Sean, who am I talking to?"

"This is Levi, I'm one of the Elders of Atlantis. I want you to leave the trucks and make your way down to the water, everyone is on the sub. Two Navy Seals will take you to the sub that is sitting on the bottom of the bay.

"We had to get the Commandos to the entrance and the thermo unit and send them down to Atlantis, then destroy the thermo unit and seal the entrance forever. There were just too many troops and tanks coming at them, they would have been run over in just seconds. You both will now go to Israel to fight against the Antichrist with all your friends on Sub 101."

Sandra and Meg were taken from the airport as soon as they got off the plane at Cairo by Special Forces from Israel. They both are now safe from the intruders, in Israel.

Megan let them think they had broken her and gave them lots of information. She was then taken from the prison to the Antichrist's headquarters. Before the car got to the headquarters, it was stopped by Special Forces from Israel. She was taken by the underground to Israel. All the people were now safe and in God's hands.

The three subs, 101, 103 and 104 made it to Israel and will stay there to fight the Antichrist. Time has gone by, it is now the last three and a half years of the Tribulation.

Everyone that came on the subs to Israel went to Tel Aviv-Yafo Sourasky Medical Center for treatment.

Date - October 23, 2021

The Last Three & A Half Years Are Here

The book of Revelation in the Bible will tell you what's going to happen next.

The Antichrist has been waiting for this day so he can attack Israel and kill the two Prophets and 144,000 priests. They were sent out by God and Israel to bring the gospel of Jesus Christ to every country in the world during the first half of the Tribulation. These two great Prophets caused it not to rain and brought plagues onto all the people who wouldn't stop sinning and accept Jesus as their god. He couldn't kill them until their time was up.

The Jewish temple is finished. The news of its completion was on every major news station. Jewish people and the Gentiles started coming from all over the world to worship God and see this new temple. Oct 31, 2021 was going to be the day of celebration. All world leaders were invited, some refused to come as they hated the Jews and wanted them killed and the temple destroyed. "Jihad, jihad," they yelled and started riots in Muslim countries and where they had large mosques.

At about the same time, all the large banks in the world, which were being controlled by the tall colored leader of the Common Market, told all their customers to turn all their money in by the end of November and pick up their debit card with their personal number on the card.

"You won't be able to buy or sell anything without your card. Money will be worthless after November. By the end of 2021 all the citizens of the world must turn in their money and get their debit cards. All citizens will be told what bank to go to, to pick up their card and turn their money in for credits on their debit card."

Just before the last seven years and the Tribulation, the man running the computers and the banks worldwide was shot in the head and survived the major head wound. This man was the President of the ten nations of the European Common Market. He lay in a hospital bed for three months. He was declared brain dead and the plug had been pulled off the respirator. The next day he died of his wounds. The doctors went to the waiting room and sadly told his wife the bad news. When his wife and the two girls went into the room to say goodbye, he sat up and asked them why they were crying. The word of this recovery from death spread around the world. It was a miracle given by God to save this man.

He was a tall colored man; many people had said that he was from Kenya. All the Arab countries wouldn't take his debit card unless he broke his seven-year treaty with Israel and helped them attack Israel.

He calls all the Arab nations and tells them of his plan to take over their temple and turn it back over to them. He also tells them that he is one of them and wants to kill every Jew and rid the world of them. "I'm the Antichrist!" he declares. Sent by Allah, to clear the world of the unbelievers.

The next day he attacks Israel with a large force and the Arab nations joined forces with him. Israel puts up a good fight but is losing ground to this large force. They are driven out of Jerusalem in just five days and the Antichrist takes over the temple of God.

He sits down on the throne and acts like he is God. He has the two Prophets and the 144,000 priests killed. He puts the two great Prophets' bodies out in the street and has his news people show the world they are dead and that he has killed them.

For three and a half days they party and send gifts to each other for the ones that tormented them are dead. After the three and a half days, the two Prophets stand on their feet and are taken up into the clouds. The cameras weren't turned on when this was happening.

Israel calls on the United States, their last friend, to come and help drive these people from their land and their temple. The U.S. sends four aircraft carriers and troop transporters to help out.

"We will be sending troop ships and supplies. Our satellites have been watching them build up troops in Egypt for some time now. They have been after some people that claim to be from Atlantis."

"Whoever they were, they seem to be gone from the face of the Earth. Maybe they were part of the Christian Rapture."

"We will be ready to attack on November 2."

The intruders on Israeli soil were all around the temple, when wave after wave of planes from the four carriers stopped them dead in their tracks.

Then from behind the intruders came thousands of Jeeps with rocket launchers and heavy 50-caliber machine guns tearing into the troops and tanks. They were hard to hit as they raced up and down ranks of troops.

In the mass confusion, the intruders were shooting at each other. The battle went on for two weeks; on Nov 17 they retreated to their ships in Egypt. Some of his troops went overland through Lebanon and Syria. He went back to his headquarters in Rome licking his wounds.

The Antichrist hated the United States for helping the Jews. He was very vengeful and vowed to make the U.S. sorry they had helped them. He would have been standing in their temple and would have driven them off their land that they claimed was theirs, this land that they took by force from the Muslims back when David was their King.

"The United States will pay with their lives, I will destroy their country from shore to shore, I will set it on fire."

Atlantis had opened the tunnel in Egypt and had sent all the Jeeps up from Atlantis. The following people were in charge of a hundred Jeeps each. They were all taken to the Jeeps in Egypt.

Volunteers were asked to step forward. Not one single person went backwards.

(The Desert Fox Team)

Liam, DF 1.----Sean, DF 2.----Johnny, DF 3.----Tom, DF 4.----Brady, DF 5.----Wesley, DF 6.----Samuel, DF 7.----Al, DF 8.----Dwayne, DF 9.----Morgan, DF 10.----Harrison, DF 11.----Sandra, DF 12.----Megan, the back up driver and gunner for Sandra.

Every Jeep had two Commandos, just in case one was wounded or killed. All the other Jeeps were manned by Commandos. This was one hell of a fighting force.

When the Antichrist got back to Rome he called all the nations in the Common Market and told them to get all the troops ready to go to Israel. He then talked to the Russian President and said it was time to hit the United States.

"They can't stop you. You can destroy them in one day. They have a weak President who only wants to talk peace. He has given up most of his atomic weapons and has destroyed most of them per your agreement of one for one. They never checked on you, they just took your word on how many you destroyed. I have all my troops getting ready to attack Israel just as soon as you hit the U.S."

Date - November 20, 2021

The President of Russia called the President of the Common

Market.

"We are not ready to attack the U.S. at this time."

"Put your troops on standby."

"The U.S. President wants to play war games with our submarines. He wants to put his subs in our waters, he says we won't be able to find them."

"If you find a sub, that's a kill. The one with the most kills will win the war games."

"He wants to put all his submarines around our country first, to show that his subs are far superior to ours and can't be found."

"He said his subs will stop any nation from thinking about attacking the United States. He said after 15 days they will all surface at one time so you can see that they are far superior to yours."

"We will put on a good show for them, we won't find any of their subs at that time. We have just made a space satellite that can put a hidden electronic beacon on their subs, but they must be on the surface to do that. Then we will know right where they are and can take them out all at one time just before we attack the United States. In 15 days we will then put our subs around their country. We will let them think they found all our subs, but we will keep about a hundred other subs hidden off their coast.

"He will tell the American people all about the war games, that they don't have to worry about Russia or any other nation attacking them, as it would be suicide for them to do so, that just a few of their subs can take out any nation.

"We will then set up all his subs to be hit at one time, as we will know where each one is hiding. As our subs get close to their subs, they will remember the war games, they will think they can't be seen. It will be over in just a few minutes and all of their subs will be heading for the bottom.

"That's when our subs and land based missiles will be launched at every major city in the U.S. You're right we can destroy them in one day.

"In about 30 days as you requested, I will attack the U.S. and their subs all at the same time. A good day to attack would be one when most of the military will be home."

Date and Time
December 25, 2021
Time 6 AM in WA, D.C.

"Get your people ready to attack Israel at that time and on that date. We will destroy both of them at the same time."

The date finally came and Russia sank all the subs and set America on fire from coast to coast with atomic bombs from her subs and land based missile sites. A few missiles came from American missile sites and hit Moscow and some other cities. It was a small price to pay for what they did to the U.S.

Israel was again under attack by the Antichrist. His large military force drove right into Jerusalem and again he took over the temple of God. Russia took over all the European countries that weren't part of the Common Market; she then set her sights on South America.

The Antichrist was now working out of his new headquarters, the temple of God. He was controlling all the countries with his computers. Everyone in the world, including Russia had to turn their money in and get their new debit card.

He was right, no one in the world could buy or sell without this card. Russia was going around the world taking over countries and the Antichrist was making them take his mark.

Israel and the Desert Foxes were keeping the Antichrist from advancing any further than Jerusalem. Planes were still coming in from the last American ships out in the Mediterranean and taking out their tanks and troops.

The Antichrist had the Russian subs take out all the American ships.

The Israeli troops and the Atlantis forces had to hide in the mountains as they were now all alone. There they would fight hit and run tactics all through the last three and a half years.

Time went by slowly, while Russia and the Antichrist took over the world.

The Antichrist was in the temple saying he was God. All people of the earth must worship the image of the beast and take his mark or die. His church will go about the world giving everyone the mark or cutting their heads off.

There were large earthquakes, poisoned seas, lakes and rivers were turning red from the dying animals, unfit to drink, plagues one after another, sores all over one's body.

The Russian President had enough of the Antichrist, who couldn't even cure the sores on his own body. Some God he was, the President could see right through him; he was nothing but a world dictator. It was wrong to have destroyed the United States. The Antichrist just wanted them out of the way so he could convert everyone to his religion. He was sitting over there in his temple collecting all the riches and oil from all the nations around him.

The President of Russia told his generals to attack the Antichrist and take over all the land and the temple and drive him out of Israel. Russia came with their armies and drove them out of Israel. The Antichrist and his troops were no match against the Russian armies and they retreated back to Rome.

Date - December 15, 2024

The Antichrist goes to China to talk with the leaders of China, as they have been real good friends.

"If you will help me destroy the Russian army that has taken over Israel, I will give you and your people any land you desire in the world, but the land of the Common Market countries and the land of Israel. These I must keep for myself."

"I will be glad to help you, Russia has always been against the people of China and has turned its back on the Communist Party."

"I will go around the world and gather armies from all the nations and bring them to Armageddon. The river Euphrates has dried up and you will be able to cross it with your armies and the armies of your allies. We will meet there on April 1, 2025. It will take that long to move all our armies. Your army alone is over 200 million strong and with all the support people it will take you that long to get into position."

Date - April 1, 2025
ARMAGEDDON

The armies are now gathered at Armageddon and they attack the Russian army. This battle will last for 24 days.

The armies of the world will be too much for the armies of Russia. Only one out of six will get out of this valley alive. The rest will be slaughtered to the last man; the ones that do make it will flee for their lives back to Russia. Blood will run through the valley as deep as a horse's bridle.

The Antichrist will again be the leader of the world, but it will be short lived. He will turn towards Jerusalem with all his armies, but he will never reach the temple again. The seventh angel and God will destroy his army at the gates of Jerusalem.

"There came a great voice out of the temple of heaven." It was God saying, "It is done."

Date - April 25, 2025

Sea of
Azov

Black Sea

ROATIA

a

Bosphorus

Strait of
Otranto

ALBANIA

Sea of
Marmara

Thracian
Sea

GREECE

Aegean Sea

Dardanelles

TURKEY

Ionian
Sea

t of
sina

Myrtoan
Sea

Gulf of
Antalya

S E A

Sea of Crete

Crete

Cyprus

Levantine Sea

LEBANON

Libyan Sea

ISRAEL

Gulf of
Sidra

LIBYA

EGYPT

Red
Sea

About the Author

Phil Gregoire served in the military in Cuba during the 1950s. He was raised on a farm in North Dakota and went to school in Minnesota just across the river. He says to say the names of the states with an accent because, "it sounds better."

The river was the border line between the two states. It seems like he spent about the same amount of time at each location.

He didn't like school and he didn't like farming so he went fishing. That was something he was really good at.

This big priest who played football for the Fighting Irish would come down to the river and drag him back too school. Phil tried to run once, but he never tried that again. There were willows by the river, if you were ever hit by one all the way back to school, you wouldn't run away either. That was the end of the fishing during school hours. That was just one of many lesson learned, some the hard way, some the easy way.

Phil believes in Jesus Christ and that he will soon be coming back to this Earth and that he carries a bigger stick then a willow. So pay attention to the "Ten Commandments" since those willows really hurt, just think what that big stick is going to do. The story in the book tells you how to save your soul; it's yours and yours alone so don't just give it away.

THERE ARE TWO CHRISTS WHO WANT YOUR SOUL.
THE ANTI- CHRIST AND JESUS CHRIST.

Enjoy the book; it was started twenty-six years ago and put on a shelf until 2016. As you can see it's done. Better late then never.

God Bless you and your loved ones.

Phillip Gregoire

Made in United States
Orlando, FL
05 June 2025